ON THE ROAD

#4

MAKING WAVES

Stephanie Doyon

Aladdin Paperbacks

First Aladdin Paperbacks edition August 1999

Text copyright © 1999 by Stephanie Doyon

Aladdin Paperbacks
An imprint of Simon & Schuster
Children's Publishing Division
1230 Avenue of the Americas
New York, NY 10020

Designed by Steven M. Scott
The text for this book was set in Wilke Roman.
Printed and bound in the United States of America
2 4 6 8 10 9 7 5 3 1

Library of Congress Catalog Card Number: 99-64467
0-689-82110-7 (pbk.)

For Clodagh and Aisling

How are we doing over here?"

I tear my eyes away from my leather travel notebook, pen still poised over the pages, and self-consciously try to cover the writing with my arm. "Fine," I answer, clearing my throat. The smiley train attendant's eyes drop down to the notebook, then back up to my face. The name tag on her navy blazer says, TINA.

"Welcome aboard the *California Zephyr*," she says, her voice as smooth as milk. "May I see your ticket, please?"

I fish it out of the seat pocket and hand it to her.

"Miranda Burke . . . you'll be with us all the way to Oakland, Miranda?" Tina asks, inspecting the ticket. "Is this your first time visiting the Bay Area?"

"Yes," I answer dully, my arm still protectively covering the notebook. "I'm visiting my best friend."

"Whereabouts?"

"San Francisco."

Tina's eyes squint with just the right amount of expertly trained approval. "There are pillows in the overhead compartments, and blankets may be purchased in the café car for ten dollars. I would recommend getting one—the train can get chilly overnight."

"I'll keep that in mind," I mumble, anxious to return to my journal.

"Let me know if there's anything else I can do for you," she says.

With a weak smile, I wait for her to turn her back before I continue. *Where was I?* I wonder, glancing out the window at the snowy-white peaks of the Rockies. As the last remnants of Denver fade to the east, the creative burst that hit me while I was waiting for the train starts to wane a little. It was the oddest thing, really. I was curled up in a ball on the end of one of those benches, doing everything I could not to think about Dustin, when I suddenly just decided to write it all down—hopefully putting it on paper would help me figure out what I was feeling. So, I picked up a pen, and the words unraveled on the page like a ball of string. And I haven't been able to stop since.

The late afternoon sun begins to slide behind the mountains, darkening the coach car of the superliner. A few people turn on their overhead reading lights, the focused yellow beams hitting the tops of their heads like mini-spotlights. My eyes are heavy and tired from the strain of writing and the roller-coaster ride of emotions that started early this morning at the Denver airport. I close the notebook and resolve to just chill out until dinner.

"Excuse me, ladies and gentlemen," Tina's voice comes over the loudspeaker. "The trivia contest is about to begin for anyone who is interested. Whoever can answer the most trivia questions correctly wins an official *Zephyr* travel mug! If you want to play along, please raise your hand and the attendants will be sure to get a question sheet to you."

As soon as she announces the prize, a bunch of eager hands shoot up in the air—mine is not one of them. What do I want a cheesy mug for? I swear, people get excited over anything free. It doesn't matter what the prize is—Tina could be giving away a can of lard and they'd still be killing each other for it.

While the attendants pass out trivia sheets, my eye catches a familiar profile in one of the aisle seats toward the front of the car. *Wait a minute . . . isn't that . . . ?* I lean forward a little and squint, but he turns around again before I can get a good look. *Nah, I must be hallucinating . . . it couldn't be . . .*

Or could it?

Keeping myself half-hidden behind the seat in front of me, I spy on the back of the guy's head, waiting for him to turn to the side again and either confirm my suspicions or hopefully prove me wrong. The guy lowers the seat tray in front of him and leans over the trivia questions, occasionally scratching the back of his neck with the end of his pen. It seems like days pass before he makes any promising movements, then all of a sudden he waves his hand in the air to get the attention of one of the car attendants. They talk for a minute or two, then the attendant points to the back of the car, her eyes grazing the top of my head. Turning around completely, he follows her gaze, his face finally coming into full view.

Oh, man . . . I groan, hunkering down so he doesn't see me. *I knew it was him . . . talk about weird luck. . . .*

I steal another quick peek, but this time, to my horror, he's out of his seat and coming right down the aisle toward me. Dread oozes from the very bottom of my stomach, spreading out to the tips of my nerve endings. In a panic, I double over and squeeze my head between my knees, like an airplane passenger preparing for impact, then cover my head with a pillow. I stare at the floor, waiting for him to walk by, my heart pounding in my ears.

Seconds later, a pair of white and blue basketball sneakers come into my limited range of view on the red aisle. Instead of continuing past me like I hoped they would, the sneakers slow down, then halt right next to my seat. *Keep on going,* I silently plead, *just keep on going . . .*

"Are you all right?" he asks me. "Are you sick?"

4

"I'm fine . . . ," I say in a squeaky voice from beneath the pillow.

Despite my incredible acting job, he doesn't seem convinced. "Should I call an attendant?"

"No . . . ," I squeak again. "Don't worry about me. Just go on ahead."

I watch as the toes of his sneakers turn toward the woman sitting across the aisle from me. "Do you think she's going to be okay?" he asks her.

"I don't know," the woman says, sounding a little suspicious. "She was fine just a minute ago."

He waits a second longer, shrugging, I suppose, then continues on to the back of the train car. When I'm sure I'm in the clear I sit up again, my face all hot and clammy and my hair going in a thousand different directions. Everyone within a two-seat radius is looking at me like I'm a psychopath.

"Whew!" I exhale loudly, stretching my arms over my head. "Just thought I'd practice a little yoga—that felt fantastic!"

I take one last look behind me just in time to see him close the door to the bathroom behind him. Cool—that ought to give me a couple of minutes, anyway. I bound into action like a loaded spring, scooping up my notebook and backpack. In ten seconds flat I've got all my stuff together, heading for the door at the front of the car.

I am *so* out of here.

The observation deck is fairly empty, which is pretty surprising because as far as I'm concerned, it's the nicest part of the train. With the curved glass ceiling, you get a spectacularly unobstructed view of the mountains and plenty of sunlight, or what is left of it, anyway. There are board games up here, if you're into that sort of thing, and I heard someone say they're even going to show a movie later. It sounds like staying here for the rest of the trip won't be so bad after all. At least it's better than the alternative.

There's a good reason why I freaked when I saw that guy. His name is Mike Hartley, and he's a friend of my brother's from high school who used to hang around our house all the time when I was growing up. I haven't seen him in over a year, since Jay left for college, and I'd like to keep it that way.

As far as I could figure out, Mike had two totally different personalities. To the entire student population of Greenwich High, he was extremely outgoing and likable. Guys knew they could always count on Mike for a pickup game after school or to tell them where the cool parties were going to be on the weekend. The girls loved to give him bear hugs and always described him as a "sweetheart." He was even a favorite among the teachers, not for his stellar academic performance so much as for his sharp sense of humor and natural charm. I'll admit, I was suckered in by Mike just as much as everyone else was—that is until I finally had a chance to see a side of him that made me change my mind for good.

The day Mike turned on me it was the beginning of August, a few weeks before I was about to start high school. The three of us—Jay, Mike, and me—were hanging out by the pool. We were all having a pretty good time, or so I thought, with Jay and Mike giving me the inside scoop on all I needed to know to survive my first day of high school. In the middle of our conversation, Jay went into the house to get something to drink and as soon as the slap of the screen door sounded, Mike's charming personality did a complete 180.

"My biggest fear is that I won't be able to find all my classes," I told him, continuing our conversation as I floated lazily on my pink air mattress, "or that I'll trip going up the front steps. I don't want to do anything that will draw attention to myself."

"Don't worry," Mike said, scowling. "No one's going to notice you, anyway."

The change in him was so sudden and so noticeable, it nearly sent me flying off my air mattress. "What do you mean by that?" I asked.

Mike leaned back in the lounge chair, hands confidently propped behind his head. "Don't take yourself so seriously. You're just a freshman. You'll blend into the woodwork just like the rest of them."

"Thanks a lot," I answered, trying unsuccessfully to disguise my hurt feelings.

"It's the truth."

"Fine, it's the truth. You don't need to rub it in."

Mike smirked at me from behind his shades. Usually, he was kind and thoughtful, but suddenly he was all attitude. "You know what? I take that back. You couldn't possibly blend into the woodwork with that hair of yours."

I remember the distinct ripple of panic that shot through me at that moment. "What's wrong with my hair?" I asked him.

"It's *very* red."

"Is there something wrong with red?"

Mike shrugged. "It's distinctive."

Like practically every girl my age, I was totally insecure with all aspects of my physical appearance, especially my red hair. Mike knew it, too.

"Have you found out when your lunch period is?" he asked, coming over to the edge of the pool to dip his toes.

"I don't know." I sat up on the mattress and let

myself sink down into the water a little. "I think my schedule said twelve-thirty."

Mike winced, then made a clicking sound with his tongue. "Oooh. Late lunch. That's too bad."

Of all the things I had been worrying about, the problems of lunch had never even occurred to me. I took in a shaky, nervous breath and tried to draw up enough courage to find out what he was talking about. "What's wrong with late lunch?"

"Well, the food is all cold and dried up for one," he said with an air of absolute authority, "and you can never find a place to sit."

"I'm sure I'll find a seat *somewhere*," I argued, my tone falling halfway between a statement and a question. "Not *all* the seats can be taken."

Mike dragged his toe along the surface of the water and splashed me. "Of course there are empty seats—but the upperclassmen don't let the freshmen sit with them. Sometimes they'll even make you sit on the floor so they can drop table scraps on you like a dog."

"You're lying," I said with a scowl, my insides falling apart.

Thankfully, Jay showed up at that point, carrying a couple of bottles of iced tea. Mike's antagonistic side dissolved, and his bright smile reemerged. But I was still stinging from his comments.

"Mike was just telling me about lunch," I complained, dunking my head in the water to make my red hair look dark.

Mike laughed and returned to his lawn chair. "I was telling her about how great it is to be able to choose what you want to eat. The food's not that good, but at least you can pick the lesser of two evils."

"He's right." Jay laughed. "It's just like we've been telling you, M, you have nothing to worry about. You're going to love high school."

I was about to tell my brother what he *really* said, but Mike shot me a dark look and I kept my mouth shut. The rest of that summer was torture for me, spending many afternoons cruising the hair dye displays at Robert's Pharmacy and lying awake at night trying to think of places I could eat my lunch if the cafeteria was full. Mike's split personality continued on throughout the rest of high school, coming and going depending on if anyone else was ever around. For a long time, I was convinced he had it in for me—he seemed to take an enormous amount of pleasure in finding my insecurities and plucking them one by one like the strings of a harp. I did my best to ignore everything he said, but when someone continually puts you down, no matter what you do, the bad stuff has a way of seeping in, anyway.

I know all this stuff with Mike happened a long time ago, and maybe I shouldn't make such a big deal of avoiding him, but here's how I look at it: When I was a kid and Mike was hanging around the house, making fun of me, I didn't think there was anything I could do about it. Now that I'm older, I can see now that I don't have to talk to anyone who makes me feel bad about myself even if they're standing right in front of me. It's up to me to make that choice for myself.

And the way things stand right now, I don't ever want to see his face again.

A voice comes over the train loudspeaker, soft but sudden enough to startle me. "In approximately five minutes, we will be entering the Moffat Tunnel. The tunnel is 6.2 miles and will take about ten minutes to go through. During this time no one will be allowed to cross between cars, in order to prevent exhaust from entering the train. If you would like to move to another part of the train, please do so now."

A few people shuffle in and out while the observation deck attendants turn off all the blowers that pull in air from the outside. I lean back in my seat, comforted by the fact that I won't have to worry about running into Mike for at least the next ten minutes.

"The Moffat Tunnel crosses the Continental Divide at an altitude of 9,239 feet," the voice continues. "Here's a fact that you *trivia* buffs will be interested in. Before its construction in 1927, trains needed about five hours to cross the Divide, climbing to an astonishing height of well over 11,000 feet!"

A few moments later, the scenery disappears as we slip into the black tube. My reflection appears before me, warped by the curve of the glass. I look haggard, tired, and in desperate need of a shower. My hair is stringy, and my eyes look puffy and dark, almost ominous in this strange, shadowy mirror. The car is quiet, and in this empty moment with nothing to do or think about or even look at, I can feel my heart starting to hurt again. Maybe *hurt* isn't the right word. Actually, it feels more like it's missing. But it's not really missing, either, because I know exactly where it is: with Dustin, in an airplane somewhere over the Atlantic, on its way to London. I've never broken up with someone before, so I don't really know how this all works. I still have questions. Like, if you give your heart to someone, do you ever get it back in one piece? Or do you collect it in bits, a little at a time, and have to put it back together yourself?

I hug my knees to my chest, endlessly twirling around my finger the silver rope ring Dustin gave me just before he boarded the plane, remembering the devastated look on his face when I told him I wouldn't be going with him to Europe after all. It had been a spontaneous decision, made with the same carelessness as when I originally told him I would go. Now here I am, on my way to California, and life is happening so fast, I can hardly keep up with it.

This new wave of insecurity leaves me hungering

for an escape. I lunge for my notebook and flip through furiously, searching for the page where I had stopped. When I reach it, the aching begins to subside a little. I uncap my pen and start to write.

I keep writing until long after we exit the tunnel, my creative flow interrupted only by the gnawing pangs of hunger I've been ignoring for who knows how many miles. Collecting my stuff again, I head for the dining car, but once I see the menu prices, I quickly turn on my heels and head for the café car instead. The last time I checked my wallet, things were looking pretty grim. I don't know how it all disappeared so quickly—I thought I had been careful. If I didn't have my dear friend Chloe to stay with in San Francisco, I'd be in serious trouble right now, or at the very least I'd have to live off my emergency credit card, which definitely wouldn't go over too well with the parental units. As soon as they got the first bill, I can almost guarantee my dad would be on the next flight to San Francisco to personally drag me home.

At the snack counter I buy a shrink-wrapped tuna salad roll and a ginger ale. I debate whether or not to buy a ten-dollar blanket, like Tina suggested, but finally decide not to on principle alone. If it gets chilly, I can pile on more clothes or cover myself with the sheetsack Dustin had Kirsten and me make for our stay at the youth hostel.

Dustin . . . what are you doing right now?

"Are you okay?"

I give my head a shake and force myself back to reality, trying to focus on the pudgy woman behind the café counter who is talking to me. "What?" I ask vaguely, wondering how long I had drifted off.

"I asked you if you were okay. You were sighing really loudly, like this—" She raises her rounded shoulders as high as her ears, drawing in a deep breath, then exhales wearily, as if the weight of the world is bearing down on her.

I curl my upper lip. "I did that?"

"You sure did, honey," she says. "Anything you want to talk about?"

Grabbing my dinner and a stack of napkins, I shake my head. "I'm just hungry . . . it's been a long day."

"Tell me about it," the counter lady says.

I get the feeling she's in the mood to start a conversation, but before it gets any further I shuffle off to a booth in the back, taking the seat that faces the door at the front of the car. If, by some chance, Mike comes in through the front, I'm only a few steps away from an escape out the back, into the sleeper cars.

I put my stack of paper napkins to the left of the sandwich, then crack open the ginger ale and take a sip. I've never liked eating alone in public—without the distraction of a companion, I always feel like someone's watching me make a pig out of myself. Delicately, I peel back the sandwich wrapping and take a small bite.

"Pardon me—may I sit here?"

I look up from my sandwich and see a striking woman with long black hair and fair skin standing next to the booth. I'm hardly in the mood to talk to anyone, but I guess it's better than eating alone.

"Sure," I say, covering my mouth with a napkin.

"Thank you," the woman says, sliding into the seat across from me with her cup of coffee.

I stare down at my sandwich, taking nibbles from it here and there, staying firmly behind the invisible line I've psychologically drawn down the center of the table. In my peripheral vision I watch her unzipping her leather purse and pawing at its contents as if she's looking for something.

"Oh, dear," she says as if to herself. Then, looking at me, she says, "Perchance you have a pen I could borrow?"

Perchance? Who talks like that? The lilt of her voice seems vaguely familiar, but I can't really pinpoint her accent. I'll admit I'm intrigued, but not enough to get entangled in a minefield of small talk.

"Here," I say dryly, handing her my pen.

The woman gives me a pleasantly reserved smile and begins jotting notes in the tiny, spiral-bound book she retrieves from her purse. As I quietly munch on my sandwich, I can't help noting the intense look of concentration that wrinkles her brow and the speed with which she fills page after page. Every few minutes she looks up from her writing and stares out the window, seemingly immersed in thought.

"Pardon me again," she says in between sips of coffee. "When we were going through the tunnel, do you recall how long the announcer said it was?"

At last I'm able to place the accent—she sounds Irish. "I think they said 6.2 miles," I answer, draining the last of my soda.

"6.2 . . . that would be about 9.9 kilometers, wouldn't it?"

"I don't know the metric system," I say bluntly, gathering up the napkins and plastic wrap, ready to make a quick exit. We're still not engaged in a full conversation—there's time to get out gracefully. Before I leave, though, I can't resist one final crack. "You're playing that trivia game, huh? Are you doing it for the mug or for the love of competition?"

"Oh, I'm not playing the game," the woman says with a gentle laugh. "I'm gathering information for the project I'm working on. I'm a writer."

"Oh, yeah?" I slide back into the booth. "What kind of stuff do you write?"

The woman puts her notebook down. "I'm working on a travel guide at the moment—rather dry work, I'm afraid. When time permits, I dabble a little in fiction." She gives me a wry smile. "My name is Aislinn, by the way."

"Nice to meet you, Aislinn. I'm Miranda." I feel my cheeks redden with the regret. "This is my first long-distance train trip," I offer as explanation for my previously cool demeanor.

Aislinn takes my behavior graciously in stride, holding no grudge. "It's grand, isn't it? Even though it takes much longer, I prefer the train."

"You're from Ireland, aren't you?" I ask. "My grandparents were from Ireland."

"Where?"

"Galway."

Aislinn's blue-green eyes look at me curiously. "What's the last name?"

"Burke," I answer.

She thinks for a moment, then shakes her head. "I don't believe I know any Burkes in Galway. I'm from County Cork. Have you been?"

I shake my head. "I've never been out of the country—except to Canada, once."

"It's lovely," Aislinn says. "I'm sure you'll get there eventually. When you do, you'll have to look up the O'Driscolls—tell them you know me and they'll take good care of you."

"Just 'the O'Driscolls'?" I laugh. "Shouldn't I know the first names, too?"

"Any O'Driscoll will do," she answers, taking a sip of her coffee. "It's a small county."

I lean forward with my elbows on the table between us, trying to steal a peek at the contents of Aislinn's little notebook. "So this book you're writing—it's about train travel?"

"Not exactly," she says, tossing her thick mane

of hair over one shoulder. "I've only been hired to write about San Francisco, but I thought maybe I'd try to put together a wee bit about the *Zephyr* on the way and hopefully convince my publisher to buy that as well. Kind of a two-for-one special."

"Sounds like you have the perfect job," I say wistfully. "You get to travel all over the place and write about it. I can't imagine anything better."

In the back of my mind I conjure up this hopelessly romantic vision of me and Dustin spending our lives circling the globe—him conquering the world's highest peaks, and me capturing the essence of each place on paper. Just the thought of it makes me shudder with bliss.

Aislinn smiles modestly. "I do enjoy it, but constant travel and deadlines can be a bit of a drain. I fancy I'd rather stay put and work on my novel."

"The strangest thing happened to me today . . . ," I start, almost subconsciously. I feel slightly detached from my own body, as if I'm off to one side, watching myself speak. "I had this sort of traumatic emotional event this morning, and the next thing I know, a few hours later, it felt like this dam broke inside of me and I suddenly have this urgent need to write. I just had to write and write and write . . . that's never happened to me before."

"Quite an amazing feeling, isn't it?"

"I suppose," I say. "Mostly it's just weird. Then again, nothing in my life has been normal since the beginning of summer."

"So I guess writing is a new discovery for you?"

"Well, yeah . . . pretty much," I answer, snapping the metal tab off my soda can. "Except little things like keeping a diary—I've been doing that pretty steadily since I was eight—and school papers. I've always done really well in English class, but I think that's because I love to read so much. And oh, yeah—and I went through this really big poetry-writing phase when I was four-teen—but that doesn't really count, because every teenager goes through that."

Aislinn studies me with the same intense look she gave her notebook. "Let's see—you love reading, you've been writing from a young age, you think it's the perfect job, and you've never considered being a writer?"

"I don't know . . . " The absurdity of it hits me, leaving me feeling slightly confused. "I probably thought about it a long time ago, but gave up on the idea because I knew I'd never make a living at it."

"If you're not the kind of person who needs a lot of material wealth, you can certainly make a decent life for yourself," Aislinn says. "And you can always take another job if you need a bit extra to put food on the table. It can be done."

Aislinn's words resonate clearly inside me, lifting a burden I didn't even know I was carrying. *Miranda Burke, writer.* Do I even dare to imagine it?

"Tell me what it's like—" I say, leaning in even closer. "You know, to be a writer."

Suddenly the door at the front of the car slides open for probably the thousandth time since I've been sitting here, and before I even look up, I instinctively know it's Mike. *Why now?* I grumble silently to myself. *Don't you have trivia questions to answer?*

Aislinn, who has no idea what's going on, closes the notebook and demurely folds her hands on the table. "First of all, I don't think it's nearly as glamorous as—"

"I'm sorry, Aislinn, but I have to go," I mutter quickly as I jump to my feet. "It was really nice talking to you, best of luck with everything."

She looks at me in confusion, murmuring a weak good-bye. I feel bad and want to apologize again, but there's no time. Holding my pack like a shield in front of my face, I disappear out the back door.

I've been standing here in the vestibule between cars for what feels like days, shivering my butt off while Mike takes his sweet old time ordering a hot dog. Through the rectangular window I see him reaching into every blasted pocket of his cargo pants to find the exact change, chatting it up with the lady behind the counter, skillfully loading on the ketchup and mustard with such precision, you'd think he was going to present it to the queen of England. He's so slow, it's almost comical, as if he knows I'm out here waiting for him to leave and he's taking his time just to annoy me. If I wasn't standing here cold, bored out of my skull, I'd probably be laughing.

Instead of taking his snack back to coach, like I'd hoped, Mike plops down in a booth near the door, facing me. I grumble silently to myself, feeling like a trapped rat. It's hopeless.

I'm not about to stand here and watch you eat, I say silently, rubbing my chilly arms. *Even I have my limits.* Sliding my enormous pack onto my back, I move on into the sleeper car to kill time while poky Mike has his dinner.

The hallway of the sleeper is narrow and quiet, with the private compartments to the left of me and train windows on the right. It seems as though most of the people have gone to dinner, or maybe they're all holed up in the luxury of their private quarters, glad they don't have to mingle with the riffraff in coach. I frown at the exclusive row of numbered doors, wishing I could see what it's like on the other side.

I bumble down to the end of the hallway, then turn around again, my pack digging sharply into my shoulders every time it bumps against the wall. I shift the weight from one side to the other to get more comfortable, struggling to keep my balance in the moving train. Falling back slightly, I feel the wall give beneath the strain of my weight.

Oh, my God, I think in panic as I grab a side rail to steady myself. *I broke something.*

When I turn around to survey the damage, though, instead of seeing a huge hole in the wall like I'd imagined, I notice that I simply pushed open the door of one of the private compartments. Instinctively, I start to shut the door, when my hand suddenly freezes.

The door's already open, I reason. *What would be the harm in taking a little peek?*

Slowly, inch by inch, I swing the door wider and put one eye up to the crack. The sliver of a view hardly shows anything at all, so I push it open even further, until it's just wide enough for me to stick my head in.

No one's there.

I'm not the kind of person who sneaks into forbidden places or intentionally does anything that even remotely resembles breaking rules, but I somehow now find myself standing in the middle of this private compartment, closing the door behind me. Normally, at this point, my conscience would be churning out messages of panic running up my spine, but I think missing Dustin has made me too numb to really care.

"Cool place . . . ," I say out loud, dumping my pack in the middle of the floor, much to the relief of my aching back. The powdery blue compartment is small but very efficient. There's a skinny closet on one side of the door filled with only a solitary garment bag, and on the other side there's a teeny metal sink with a teeny bar of soap and a teeny tube of toothpaste resting on the teeny metal shelf above it. Beyond the sink there's a small alcove with two doors—one has a toilet and the other a shower. A shower! I can't believe these people get showers! And I have to buy my own blanket?

The compartment window is large and smudge free, unlike the blurry, palm-printed windows in coach. Two plush royal blue recliners flank each side of a folding table. I sit down in one of them and lean back, thumbing through the complimentary train guide, which has a listing of all the great sites, a full room service menu, and instructions on how to pull the bed down from the wall. This little room is so cool—and completely Mike free— I wish I could stay in here forever. Or at least for the rest of the trip.

For about a half a second I'm tempted to pull a Goldilocks, staying here long enough to take a quick shower, brush my teeth with the mini-tube of toothpaste, and maybe take a snooze on the wall bed, but knowing how the story ends, I'd probably get caught. If Kirsten were here, she could get away with it, but not me.

I turn the chair back toward the table and put the train guide in the exact spot I found it, then I take a second or two at the sink to pat a little water on my face and smooth my hair down. When I'm done goofing around I heave my pack onto my back, hoping that I've given Mike more than enough time to scram, and I reach for the doorknob.

Just as I'm about to turn it, there's a knock on the door.

I jump away from the door as if the knob has just given me a shock.

Knock, knock, knock . . . "Mrs. Van Der Houten? Are you there?" a man calls from the other side of the door.

I stand with my hand frozen in the air, afraid to even breathe. *Don't say anything and he'll go away,* reasons a calm, optimistic voice in my head. *He wouldn't come in uninvited. . . .*

And why not? argues another, less supportive voice. *That's exactly what you did. . . .*

"Mrs. Van Der Houten?" The man knocks again, his knuckles rapping politely against the door. There is a silent pause, lasting one or two beats, then the knob slowly turns.

Blood rushes in my ears, and my eyes bulge out of their sockets as I watch the door swing open, inch by inch. There's no time to hide in the closet or the bathroom, and I'd never be able to fit my pack in there, anyway. Clenching and unclenching my fists, I stand in the doorway, rigid with fear.

The door swings open about halfway, and a well-scrubbed man in his thirties, wearing a navy train attendant's uniform, pops his head into the room. When he sees me, a startled look flickers in his eyes. It's only a matter of seconds before he regains his composure.

"Pardon me, miss, I didn't hear anyone answer," the attendant says, looking flushed. The name on his tag says BRIAN.

For the first time in several minutes, my frozen tongue loosens enough so I can speak. "That's because I didn't say anything."

"Oh . . . " Brian's voice trails off as he gives me a sidelong glance. "Mrs. Van Der Houten asked that I turn the bed down for her."

"Right," I say, smiling casually, feeling my face take on a thousand shades of red. *Do I look nervous? Does he sense that something's up?*

Brian turns his back to me and pulls the release handle on the bed. It comes out of the wall, just like it showed in the instruction book.

"Well, I'll get out of your way, then." I ease my way over to the door, struggling against every instinct in my body to turn around and run like a madwoman.

I'm about two feet from being home free when Brian looks up and says something else to me. "Mrs. Van Der Houten is one of our regular travelers, making the trip every couple of months to visit her daughter out West," he says, smoothing down the sheets and placing a foil-wrapped mint on the pillow. "In all this time, though, she's never once traveled with anybody—and if I remember right, on the roster she's alone on this trip, too. So I'm wondering what you're doing here. I don't suppose that's a mystery you could clear up for me, is it?"

I give the attendant an airheaded giggle and shrug, then turn on my heels and aim straight for the door.

"Hold on a second—" he says, his voice growing more stern by the second.

I halt in my tracks.

"What's your name?" he asks.

I chew viciously on the insides of my hot cheeks. "Miranda," I murmur.

"Miranda *what?*"

"Miranda Burke," I say, sighing.

Brian walks away from Mrs. Van Der Houten's freshly turned-down bed and crosses his arms in front of his chest with an air of newfound authority. I can tell he's loving every minute of this. The power hungry glimmer in his eye tells me that after months, or maybe even years, of putting mints on people's pillows, he's finally stumbled upon the event he's been waiting for: a chance to get an instant promotion. Something tells me my harmless snoop session might just land me into some big trouble.

"Let me see your ticket," he says, practically drooling with anticipation.

I drop my pack and fish through the front pocket. "I didn't jump the train, if that's what you're thinking," I say, handing it to him.

Brian inspects the ticket with a scrupulous eye and even holds it up to the light as if to see if it's counterfeit. "It's says here you're supposed to be in coach."

"I know," I tell him, afraid to volunteer any more information than is necessary.

He hands the ticket back to me. "Then why are you in here? You shouldn't even be in this car."

"I was trying to avoid someone," I stammer. "I turned and accidentally opened the door and wanted to take a look around. I'm sorry—I didn't mean to cause any trouble."

Brian says nothing for several seconds, arching his eyebrow skeptically at me. "You know that I can have you thrown off this train? With one phone call, I can have the authorities waiting for you in Salt Lake City."

"I'm sure you're a very powerful and influential person, Brian," I say, trying not to gag at the sound of my own voice. "That's why I'm begging you to give me another chance. It was a foolish mistake on my part—and I certainly didn't mean any disrespect to either Mrs. Van Der Houten or your fine staff."

Brian seems to thaw a little, but he's still not all the way there yet.

"This is my first real train ride, you know," I

gush, rolling my eyes like my little sister Abby. "It's a really magical experience, isn't it? You're so lucky to be able to do it every day."

Shoving his hands in his pockets, Brian shrugs. "Actually, it can get pretty monotonous. And you get so used to the vibrations of the train that you can still feel it on your days off. I used to think the scenery was nice, but you get pretty used to that, too. I think I could map out every tree and rock from Chicago to California with my eyes closed."

"That's too bad," I say sympathetically.

"And another thing. I'm sick of the smell of mint. It makes me sick."

"I can see how you'd get tired of it."

Brian grows quiet, his gaze dropping off me and onto the floor.

I put my ticket back into my pocket. "Look, Brian, I really didn't do anything wrong in here—I just wanted to peek at the rooms. I can understand if you want to turn me in, but I was kind of hoping you'd be able to overlook the situation and just chalk it up to a welcome break in the monotony."

He takes another hard look at me. "If there's anything missing from Mrs. Van Der Houten's belongings, I'll get fired."

"I didn't take anything, I swear. If something's missing, you'll know where to find me—it's not like I'm going to jump off the train or anything."

Brian taps the toe of one of his dress shoes into

the heel of the other. "Well . . ." He looks me up and down once more. "I'll have to escort you back to your seat."

"Not a problem—I appreciate your understanding," I answer. I'm so relieved, I could cry.

"I assume you realize that if we find you in the sleeper car again, you *will* be removed from the train."

"Of course," I answer. Brian carries my pack for me as we walk through the hallway on our way back to coach. To the other passengers, I suppose nothing would seem unusual about Brian carrying my pack, but it makes me feel like one of those handcuffed criminals you see on TV, when they're being escorted from a police car to the court-house. I wouldn't even be surprised if a news reporter jumped out from one of the compart-ments and shoved a microphone in my face and asked me a bunch of questions. *Yes, I was found snooping in Mrs. Van Der Houten's sleeping com-partment. No, I did not take the teeny-weeny tube of toothpaste. I have no further statements to make at this time. . . .*

Passing through the café, I'm relieved to see that Mike is nowhere to be found, with only a few balled-up napkins left behind at the booth where he had been sitting. Aislinn is gone, too.

"Which seat were you in?" Brian asks, holding the coach door open for me.

"I think it was fourteen—" My eyes scan for an

empty spot on the left side, but there's none.

"Someone's sitting there now," Brian says. He marches on down the aisle, looking for an available seat for me. "Here's a good one . . . excuse me, sir—is anyone sitting in this seat?"

There was a seat a few rows back I would've much rather preferred, but at this point I don't think I'm in much of a position to argue.

"No, it's free," the guy says, taking his jacket off the seat.

Brian heaves my pack onto the overhead rack. "There you go, Miss Burke . . . I'm sure you'll be comfortable here for the remainder of the trip."

"Right," I say, forcing a smile. "Thanks, Brian."

He shakes my hand, discreetly pressing a foil-covered mint into my palm. "Remember—Salt Lake City's not too far away."

"I won't forget."

Brian heads toward the back of the car, and I plunk down in my seat, feeling the air hiss out of my lungs like a leaky balloon. Out of the corner of my eye I can see my seatmate turning toward me, his jaw dropping in total surprise.

"Miranda—what a bizarre coincidence!"

Breathing in deeply, I scrape myself together enough to turn to him, and force the corners of my mouth upward into a crooked smile. "Hi, Mike. How's it going?"

Mike laughs and blinks hard, like he's just been hit over the head with a sledgehammer. "This is so weird! What are you doing here?"

I grip both armrests, my spine as rigid as a post. I don't want anything to do with him, and yet it feels impossible not to say anything. I answer with as few words as possible, so as not to give him fuel to ridicule me. "I'm visiting my friend Chloe Bartlett."

"I remember Chloe—blond, ballet dancer, most likely to become rich and famous," he says, summing her up pretty well. "She was over your house all the time, wasn't she? You two were best friends, right?"

"We still are." I fold my hands in my lap and pick at my hangnails. Maybe if I'm boring enough, he'll leave me alone.

"So what's Chloe doing in San Fran?"

"Studying ballet," I grunt.

Mike nods as if he's impressed. "Looks like the grads of Greenwich High are making their marks on the world." He rests his right foot on his left knee, tapping a silent drumbeat on the sole of his sneaker. "Hey, do you want the window seat instead?"

"No, *thanks*," I snap.

"You know, I knew it was you even before I saw your face," Mike says, his charming brown eyes smiling at me. What a phony. "I caught a glimpse of that red hair of yours—nobody has hair as red as yours."

Self-consciously, I push the curls off my face. "What can I say? I'm cursed."

"No way," Mike says. "It's beautiful."

I fold my arms across my chest and grit my teeth as three years of cutting remarks start shoving their way to the surface. "You didn't think it was so 'beautiful' when you knew me in high school."

Lines of confusion wrinkle Mike's forehead like he has absolutely no concept of what I'm talking about. "Yes, I did—I've always liked your hair."

"Yeah, right," I scoff. "You liked it so much that you just had to make fun of it every time you saw me."

"I didn't make fun of it, did I?"

"You sure did," I answer bitterly. "It got so bad, I almost dyed my hair black."

Mike's smile fades. "You're joking, right? I don't remember that."

I'm totally revved now. My legs are spring-

34

loaded, ready to block Mike if he even dares to try leaving his seat. This guy's going to hear me out whether he likes it or not.

"How about all the other mean things you used to say? Like the time you came up to me at the homecoming dance and said that the reason no one was asking me to dance was because I was too stuck-up? Or what about the times you used to watch me like a hawk whenever I ate something and told me I was going to get fat?"

I was hoping my rant would make Mike turn pale with embarrassment and he'd shrink down in his seat, completely mortified, but instead he just shakes his head and laughs.

"What's so funny?" I demand, tears threatening the corners of my eyes.

"I was a total moron, Miranda," he says, scratching his stubbly chin. "You couldn't have possibly taken anything I said seriously."

"How could I not? You were always breathing down my neck, ready to say something harsh when no one was around."

The laughter subsides as Mike's face grows serious. "I wasn't trying to be harsh—actually, I had a monster crush on you."

I roll my eyes. "Right—you were mean to me because you liked me so much. Oh, yeah, that makes a lot of sense."

"I wasn't trying to be mean," he says. "It's just that whenever we had a chance to be alone together, I'd get totally nervous and say something really stupid. In my head, the words sounded fine, but when they came out of my mouth, it was a disaster."

"You told me my hair was *distinctive*," I say while a war rages on in my head, deciding if I should trust that he's telling me the truth.

Mike shrugs. "Well, technically, it is. Although, *pretty* would've been a much better word choice," he says. "Look, Miranda, I can't tell you how sorry I am that I upset you like that—I really didn't mean any harm."

Stubbornly, I stare at the seat ahead of me. "You called me stuck-up."

"Maybe I was mad because you wouldn't go out with me."

"I don't remember you ever asking," I say, shaking my head.

Mike shoots me an exasperated look. "You're Jay's little sister—I couldn't just *ask* you out."

"Wait a minute, you mean all those years in school—when I thought no one was ever interested in me—it had more to do with my older brother than with my *distinctive* hair or anything else?" I ask.

Mike gives me a shrug, like this is common knowledge.

Suddenly, I'm itching to get off this train, find a phone, and call Jay. Looks like we have a lot to talk about.

Once we're over our big misunderstanding, Mike wants all the dirt on Jay. I get him all caught up on my brother's exploits, including the work he's been doing over the summer for Habitat for Humanity and the huge wedding fiasco that yours truly was responsible for. While we're talking, bits of past run-ins with Mike flash through my mind, and knowing what I know now, I can see how I might've been overly sensitive to some of his stupid remarks. It's strange seeing Mike in a new light. He's been the enemy for so long, I have to reprogram my brain to see him as a friend. Now, everything about him looks and sounds so different, I might as well be talking to a totally new person.

Tina's voice comes over the loudspeaker to announce the winner of the trivia contest. A shriek rises up from the back of the car, and a few minutes later an old woman with poofy white hair dashes up the aisle to claim the coveted plastic *Zephyr* mug. A few people reach out to shake her hand.

"Isn't it amazing what people get excited about?" I mutter as "Grandma" blows kisses at everyone like she's just been crowned Miss America.

"Tell me about it," Mike answers. "I thought I'd play along with the game, you know, just to kill some time. I got up to go to the bathroom, and when I came back, this old guy was leaning over the back of my seat, trying to read the answers I wrote down."

"You're kidding! What did you do?"

Mike shrugs. "I gave him my answer sheet. I figured if he wanted the mug that badly, he deserved to have it more than me."

"That was pretty nice of you," I say.

"See, I'm not all bad," Mike jokes, looking humble. "So I know what your brother's been up to. What's been going on with you?"

"Oh, man." I sigh. "How much time do you have?"

"The train goes all night. . . . "

"You'd need *weeks* to hear about my saga," I tell him.

Mike kicks off his sneakers and reclines his seat a little. "So give me the short version," he says. "Tell me about college—did you end up accepting to Yale?"

My body slumps against the back of my seat like a sack of dirt. You'd think I'd get used to telling people that I've postponed college, but it amazes me how much I'm still completely insecure about it. "I decided to put it off for a year or so," I say, the words sounding like a broken record by now. "I wanted to take some time to travel."

"Cool," Mike says in a completely nonjudgmental way. "Doing the whole thing by yourself?"

"Actually, I've been traveling with Kirsten Greene—remember her? She was in your class."

Mike nods slowly as it comes back to him. "Right, Kirsten Greene—dark hair, loner, most likely to deface a national monument."

"You're pretty good at that," I say, laughing.

"Four years of yearbook committee—it's like a virus you can't shake," he jokes. "So you and Kirsten have been tearing up the countryside together? I never would've pictured you two becoming friends. You're so totally different."

I lean back in the seat and kick my feet up. "We do get on each other's nerves a lot, but I think the differences help us to balance each other out. A lot of people didn't like Kirsten in school, and I know some of that was her own fault—she's always been fiercely independent."

"*Intimidating* is probably a better word," Mike adds.

"Okay, so maybe she's intimidating, but she's actually a pretty good person," I tell him. "She's taught me a lot."

Mike rises out of his seat a little and cranes his neck, scanning the car. "Where is she? How come I haven't see her?"

"Kirsten's on her way to California—we're going to meet up there," I answer. "She drove there without me because I was planning on going somewhere else instead, but I ended up changing my mind. Before we split up I begged Chloe to let Kirsten crash at her place for a couple of days, which I'm sure has been quite interesting since Chloe used to *hate* Kirsten when we were in school."

"Where did you plan on going that you changed your mind about?"

I hesitate, a pang of emptiness resonating throughout my body for the billionth time today. "I really don't want to get into it," I say, feeling myself close up tight like a clamshell.

"Sorry." Mike is kind enough not to pry.

"So"—I exhale, swallowing the lump in my throat—"I never did ask you what *you're* doing here."

"I'm checking out a few schools," he says. "I want to transfer from U. Mass."

"From the East Coast to the West Coast—that's a pretty huge jump," I say with forced cheerfulness. "Looking for a change of scenery?"

A smile lights the corners of Mike's eyes. "I met someone last summer who goes to Berkeley. Her name is Gretchen—golden-brown hair, heartbreaker, most likely to improve anything she comes in contact with. We keep visiting each other on our breaks, but it's a drag, not to mention hugely expensive. Besides, it's getting to the point where I want to be with her all the time—you know how it is. . . . "

Boy, do I know.

I turn in my seat and stare right at him. "You guys have been apart for a whole *year?*"

He nods. "Just about."

"So I guess long-distance relationships can work out after all?"

"Sure, why not?"

"That's good to know," I say, "for future reference."

Mike looks out the window, silently staring at the dusky view. He's got this soft little puppy dog face going on—pouty lips, furrowed brow, the whole deal. I can tell he's thinking about her. I can't help but wonder if Dustin's thinking about me right now, too. Is he smiling, thinking about how I let go of the rope too soon when we were practicing on the rock wall and he came crashing to the floor? Or is he looking all mushy, like Mike, thinking about our first kiss by the campfire when we were staying at that miserable little campground in the middle of nowhere?

Or maybe his face is as blank as a piece of paper, I think sullenly as the loneliness starts to creep back in, *and he's already started to forget about me.*

In the middle of the night, the train is eerily silent. As far as I can see, I'm the only one still awake, except for the car attendants who occasionally walk up and down the dimly lit center aisle like prison guards. Even Mike dozed off hours ago, curled up against the window, after graciously giving me the blanket he bought for himself in the café. Eyes wide open, I stare at the seat in front of me, anxiety coiling around the base of my spine like a boa constrictor, slowly squeezing me into a state of panic. My right foot kicks the corner of the blanket in a nervous rhythm that increases with manic frequency, my shallow breath counting out the seconds to daylight. I feel like a solo diver at the bottom of a black ocean who's just realized that the oxygen is about to run out.

In a sweaty frenzy, I throw the blanket off me and onto Mike and reach for the one thing I'm sure will keep me from completely losing it altogether—my writing book. I snap on the overhead light, my cold, numb fingers smoothing open a blank page. I try to write, but it doesn't help.

I drop the book and shake my travel buddy by the shoulders. "Hey, Mike, wake up. Sorry, but I need to talk to you. . . . "

"Huh?" he mumbles groggily.

"Wake up. I need to talk. *Please.*"

Breathing heavily, Mike turns over to my side and rubs his face until he wakes up. "Hey," he says, squinting at me, "are you crying?"

"Yeah," I whisper, my voice cracking.

Mike puts his arm around me, completely living up to his nickname of sweetheart. "What's wrong?"

"I feel like I'm losing my mind," I sniffle, burying my face in his massive shoulder. "I broke up with my first boyfriend today. I didn't want to do it—but I had to."

"Was he cheating on you?"

"No, nothing like that," I say, shaking my head. "He went to Europe for a year and asked me to go with him."

Mike strokes the top of my head. "The nerve of him!" he gently teases. "If I ever meet up with that guy in a dark alley, he'd better turn the other way and run."

In spite of the wrenching ache in my heart, I giggle. "I'm such a jerk. I told Dustin I'd go with him, and then we were just about to board the plane and I couldn't do it."

"What stopped you?"

"It feels like this happened weeks ago and not just this morning . . . ," I mumble to myself, pulling away from Mike and trying to wipe tears away from my embarrassingly puffy face. "I remember saying something about how I get airsick really easily and Dustin went ahead and bought me some motion sickness pills. Poor guy, he was just trying to take care of me, but I felt smothered. I kept thinking that this was the only time in my life that I'm really going to have the chance to rely only on myself and if I go with him, I'll lose that chance. See, I'd made this promise to myself that I was going to make it all the way to California and I wanted to keep that promise." I blow my nose so loudly, the bald guy in the seat opposite me opens his eyes for a split second before falling asleep again. "Pretty selfish, huh?"

"Actually, it sounds pretty smart to me," Mike whispers.

"You should've seen the look on his face, Mike. You'd think I'd just ripped out his heart and stomped on it." My eyes start to water again. "He said he understood, but how could he? All day long I kept replaying that conversation over and over again in my mind and it occurred to me that maybe I just didn't love him enough if I could leave him like that."

"Don't be so hard on yourself. Of course you love him. I can see it in your face." Mike reaches into his backpack and pulls out a stack of wrinkled

44

fast-food napkins imprinted with a picture of a dancing hamburger. "Think about what would've happened if you'd gone to Europe with him and weeks or months down the road you realized you needed more time on your own—what would've happened then? Don't you think it's great that you figured it out beforehand?"

I press the hamburger's smiling face to my leaky nose. "I guess."

Mike settles back in his seat. "How did things stand with you two when he left? Did you break it off for good?"

"I tried to give him my plane ticket back so he could get a refund, but he wouldn't take it," I say. "He told me it was open-ended. He said I could use it whenever I wanted."

"That's great!" Mike says. Someone from a few rows back hushes him. His voice drops to a low whisper again. "Why don't you go meet him in Europe after you visit California?"

"I thought of that, but he'll probably have found someone else by then."

"Give the guy a little credit—"

"But you should see him!" I interrupt. "He's totally gorgeous. I just know women fall for him wherever he goes—sexy, sophisticated, European women."

Mike affectionately tucks a stray curl behind my ear. "They may be sexy and sophisticated, but they're no Miranda."

"Oh, yeah, they're no match for me," I say, wrapping my words in a thick coat of sarcasm.

"Look, if you really want to stay with this guy, I know you can do it," Mike says, "but it's going to take a little faith on your part. You're going to have to trust him. You can't be worrying every second if he's with someone else, because you'll drive him and yourself crazy—believe me, I've been there. It's not fun."

I remember the mint Brian gave me and I pop it in my mouth. The sugary coolness dissolves comfortingly on my tongue. "How long did you know Gretchen before you two were separated?"

"Three months," he says. "The whole summer."

"I would think that's a decent amount of time to build a foundation for a relationship," I say. "Dustin and I have only known each other a few weeks. The time we spent together was amazing—I mean, it felt like we'd known each other forever—but how realistic is it to think we have something that can weather the strain of a long-distance relationship? It seems so complicated."

"Actually, it's pretty simple," Mike says, staring right at me. "Do you want to be with him?"

My answer comes quickly and without thought—like a natural reflex. "Yes."

Mike shrugs. "Then what are you worrying about?"

The *Zephyr* rolls into Oakland's Jack London Square early the next morning. While Mike goes to the café car to get us a couple of cups of badly needed caffeine, I slide over to the window seat and enjoy the view as the train takes a bizarre path down the middle of a busy city street, cars moving alongside us for several blocks.

"Are your friends picking you up at the station?" Mike asks, returning with our coffees.

"I left a message on Chloe's machine, so hopefully they'll be there."

"Gretchen and I could give you a ride if you needed it."

"I'll be fine, thanks," I say, taking my first hot sip. "You've done more than enough already."

Mike grins. "I suppose I owed you for all those cracks I made," he says sheepishly. "By the way, did you ever read *Call of the Wild*?"

"Yeah—a long time ago."

"Well, if you have some time to kill, you'll see these wolf tracks around the square. Follow them

47

around and you can read about the life of Jack London."

"Cool—I'll check it out," I say.

"Also, there's a huge bookstore around here, if you're interested."

I can feel my eyes opening wide. "Are you kidding? I live for bookstores."

"Somehow I knew that." Mike downs about half of his coffee in one gulp. "Don't stress if you don't get to it—there're tons of great bookstores in San Francisco."

Maybe it's knowing there are tons of bookstores waiting for me or maybe it's the fact that I'm going to finally see my best friend after being apart from her for months, but for the first time since I've left Colorado I'm finally feeling something that's bordering on excitement. It's nice to finally look ahead at things to come instead of wallowing in what happened yesterday.

At last the train comes to a halt, and over the speakers, Tina thanks us all for riding the *Zephyr* while Mike and I gather our stuff together. Every few seconds he peeks out the window, no doubt looking for Gretchen somewhere on the platform. His eyes are red and tired-looking, but his movements are loaded with a kind of kinetic energy, ready to jump into action at any second. Just like he had no idea how much he'd hurt me a long time ago, I'm sure Mike will never fully comprehend just how much he helped me last night. To him, it was just talking and some lost sleep, but to me it was a lifeline from one of the loneliest nights I've ever had. It sort of takes your breath away when you think about the effect you can have on a person's life, for good or bad, without even really being aware of it.

Standing in the middle of the platform as *Zephyr*-ites swarm around us, Mike and I scan the crowd for familiar faces.

"Any sign of her?" I ask, feeling the aggressive nudge of luggage being pushed at my heels.

"Not yet," he answers. "How about you? Do you see any of your friends?"

"They're probably in the waiting area," I tell him. "I'm going on ahead."

"Okay," Mike says, dropping his bag at his feet and stretching out his arms. "Good-bye for now, Miranda Burke—redhead, traveler, most likely to wow us all someday."

"Yeah, right," I say, laughing, stepping into his hug. "Thanks again for putting up with me last night."

He gives me a brotherly pat on the back. "Hey, why not? It made the train ride go by a lot faster. By the way, don't forget to tell Jay I said hi."

"I won't." I give Mike a grateful peck on the cheek and throw my pack onto my back before weaving through the crowd toward the waiting area. Just as I raise my hand to give him one last wave, a woman's voice rises up from the masses.

"Mike!" she shouts. "Over here!"

I look back and watch Mike's face make the amazing transition from confusion to recognition to unmistakable bliss when he finally spots Gretchen moving toward him, golden-brown hair flowing behind her. She leaps into his arms, and they spin together, kissing, like the final scene in some dramatic old black-and-white movie. They look so in love that I'd have to have a heart of stone not to be happy for them. I figure if I can't be content with my love life, someone else might as well be.

I continue on to the waiting area of the train station, hoping someone will be there for me, too.

Chloe, hi, it's me—Miranda," I shout into the phone receiver, plugging my free ear to drown out the noise of the station. "I don't know if you got the other message I left on your answering machine, but I'm here in Jack London Square—"

Before I get the rest of the message out, a hand reaches unceremoniously over my shoulder and hits the hook, breaking the line. "Excuse me, Red, you're using my phone," an antagonistic voice says from behind me. "I was here first."

Sensing a confrontation coming on, the tiny hairs on the back of my neck stand straight up. I gently replace the receiver and slowly turn around, just waiting to be decked by some two hundred–pound pay phone bully.

"S-Sorry," I stammer, one hand poised over the phone book in case I need a weapon. "I had no idea—"

Chloe snickers at my frightened look. "Gotcha," she says, a sly smile creeping across her heart-shaped face.

"You jerk!" I snap in mock anger as I give Chloe a huge hug. My arms feel as thick as tree stumps around her doelike frame. "I thought I was going to get beat up or something."

"You've always been *so* dramatic!" Chloe laughs. "It's so awesome to see you, Miranda! I can't believe you're here!"

I can hardly believe it, either. I've been imagining this reunion in my head since the day I left Connecticut, saving a little space in the corner of my brain for all the stories I wanted to tell Chloe when we were finally together again, but now that she's standing right in front of me, I can't remember a thing. It feels as though years of our lives have passed since we've been apart, and yet at the same time, she's as familiar to me as if I had just seen her yesterday. It's good to be with my best friend again. It's like coming home.

"I missed you so much, Chloe," I tell her. "It's a good thing I've been on the road, because I don't think I could've handled a summer in Greenwich without you."

"Can you believe it's been nearly three months?" She pulls back and gives me the patented Chloe once-over.

"I haven't had a shower in two days," I explain right away before she has the chance to give her analysis. My wrinkled khaki shorts and flowered tank are no match for Chloe's hot pink designer shift and delicate matching sandals. "And I was on

52

a train for twenty-four hours—just keep that in mind."

"No, no," Chloe shakes her head, "you look good. Great, even. I think this traveling thing has put the glow back in your cheeks."

You've got to hand it to Chloe, God bless her. She has a way of turning a blind eye toward those people she really likes. Had I been a stranger passing in this outfit, who knows what she would've said.

"Did Kirsten make it?" I ask, looking around.

"Oh, yeah, she's here. She got in yesterday afternoon," Chloe says, leading me toward the exit doors. "She spotted some cute guy outside selling ice cream and she's flirting with him as we speak."

I bite my lower lip. "Has everything been okay?"

"Fine so far. Better than I would've expected. She's actually pretty cool."

"See—I told you," I said, exhaling with relief.

Chloe reaches into her straw bag and pulls out a pair of shades. "So what's the story with Dustin? You chickened out at the last minute?"

"I wouldn't call it chickening out . . . I wanted to finish my trip. I felt like I still had some things I needed to do on my own first."

"Sounds like you're a liberated woman."

"I wouldn't say that, either," I answer, pulling my stringy curls into a more presentable bun. "I've been miserable ever since he left."

"Don't worry, Kirsten and I will take care of that," Chloe assures me. "We'll have a girls' night tonight—we'll give each other facials and all that."

"Facials, huh?" I answer, trying to scare up some enthusiasm. "You're right—a good mud mask is *exactly* what I need to get over Dustin."

Chloe crinkles her perfect little nose. "Don't be sarcastic—you're going to love it. You should never underestimate the power of a good cosmetic product," she says. "Besides, the point of a girls' night is to reaffirm that we can have a good time without men. I mean, who needs them, anyway?"

"I know someone who definitely does," I answer, nodding toward the ice-cream cart only a few yards away, where the blond surfer-type vendor is apparently giving Kirsten a lesson in the proper way to lick an ice-cream cone. I thought Kirsten was ready to slow down in the scamming department, but ever since she found out Vince, her old, sort-of-boyfriend in New York, moved in with someone he hardly knew, I guess her ego could use a boost.

Kirsten spots us midlick and waves us over. "Hey, guys—you want a cone? Johnny here said he'd hook us up."

"Fourteen flavors, but my personal fave is the mocha chip," Johnny says. He then scoops a plastic spoonful of it and feeds it to Kirsten in a way that makes me want to tell them to get a room.

"None for me, thanks," Chloe says, shaking her

head. "I have to watch my weight. I've got a dance audition coming up for the company. The director thinks I have a good shot at getting into the corps."

"Chloe, that's great!" I tell her.

Kirsten hands Johnny her half-melted cone and gives him a sticky farewell wave before coming over to join us. "You've got my number, right?" Johnny calls to Kirsten, seemingly unaware that vanilla fudge is dripping down his arm.

Kirsten's mouth forms a sultry pout. "It's all up here," she calls back, tapping her forehead. In a matter of seconds, I can almost see the gears switch in her brain from FLIRT to FRIEND mode. Poor Johnny. He's already a memory.

"So what's the story with you?" Kirsten asks, throwing her arm around my shoulder as we walk to the parking lot. "Tell me everything that happened with Dustin."

Rush-hour traffic on the Bay Bridge gives Kirsten and Chloe plenty of time to get caught up on the wreck that is my love life and for me to take in the panoramic views of San Francisco. Straight ahead, the densely packed skyline looms in the distance with the distinct spike of the Transamerica Pyramid, the only building I know by name, poking into the upper reaches of the atmosphere. Far to the right I can see the majestic red span of the Golden Gate Bridge stretching gracefully across the cool blue of San Francisco Bay. I've always thought that some romantic thrill would rush up through me the first time I saw it, but I'm not really feeling much of anything.

"I thought we'd do a little shopping first thing," Chloe says from the back seat as she slips out of her sandals and sticks a bare foot on the console between the two front seats. "There are some awesome shops around Union Square."

"Can we stop by your place first?" I ask, my

thighs sticking so hopelessly to the vinyl seat that I think we're exchanging molecules. "I could really use a shower."

Kirsten makes a face. "*You're* telling *me*," she teases from the driver's seat.

"Union Square is on the way," Chloe says. "If we go to my place, we have to double back." It's clear by her tone that this is not a point of discussion but a decisive fact. "There's this great little boutique that has the cutest little dresses right now on summer clearance. I haven't had a free moment this week to check it out."

"Maybe we should ask Kirsten what she wants to do," I suggest. "After all, *she's* the one who's driving. . . ."

Kirsten shrugs. "I don't care—whatever you guys want to do."

Chloe leans forward and presses her cheek against Kirsten's headrest. "Take the next left," she says decisively, putting an end to any further discussion. "So how've your mom and dad been, Miranda? Are they still in mourning over the fact that their little girl has left the nest?"

"They're slowly getting over it," I tell her. "I finally got my dad to understand that I'm not coming home in the near future and I won't be enrolling in the fall semester at Yale."

"They were still holding out hope, huh?" Chloe says, wiggling her hot pink toenails.

"You know my dad—he's never been one to

take no for an answer. It's so annoying," I say.

"It's annoying, but that's why he's so successful." Chloe directs Kirsten to a semicircular drive in front of a ritzy designer store near Maiden Lane. The woman in the silver Mercedes in front of us gets out of her car and hands the keys over to a man in a bow tie. While she goes inside the store, he moves her car over to a parking lot that's no more than twenty yards away.

"I think this is valet parking," Kirsten tells Chloe as another bow-tied attendant approaches our car. "I can just drive over to the parking lot myself and we can walk to the store."

"Why should we bother walking all the way back here?" Chloe argues. "Besides, it's only a couple of bucks."

Without further argument, Kirsten and I get out of the old beat-up Escort ourselves, while Chloe offers her hand to the valet to help her get out of the back seat. She smiles like a movie star and slips a couple of dollars into his hand. I flash a look at Kirsten, who seems to be finding the whole scene as funny as I am.

"I hope you tipped him well, Chloe," Kirsten deadpans. "That's a very expensive vehicle."

"Right—" I joke along with her, "we don't want those custom rust patches getting scratched . . . "

"Actually, I tipped him five bucks to dump it off at the junkyard," Chloe says, opening the door for us. I know she's kidding, of course, but I can't help wondering if there's an element of wishful thinking to it.

From the instant we enter the boutique, extremely well-dressed, heavily made-up saleswomen seem to materialize from every corner, descending on us like buzzards. Chloe knows them all by name and works the room as if it were a cocktail party. Kirsten casually flips through the racks, her slate-blue eyes bulging every time she looks at a price tag, while I stand off to the side, feeling horribly disheveled and out of place.

"Look at this!" Kirsten hisses. "This tank top costs two hundred dollars! That's how much I used to take home in a week when I was working as a bike messenger!"

"This place is out of control," I whisper back, showing her a four hundred–dollar silk skirt.

Chloe motions for me to come join her over by a potted palm tree that nearly reaches the ceiling. "Rhonda says she has something that's perfect for you—go ahead into the dressing room. I'll be there in a second."

"Chloe, I'm not about to buy anything here," I tell her honestly. "It's way out of my league."

"Don't get stressed out, Miranda," she answers, holding a dark blue cardigan up to my face. "We're just having fun. I thought you wanted to get Dustin off your mind."

"Sure, I'd like to not feel so bad, but I didn't say I wanted to *forget*—"

"Remember all those times we went to the mall together senior year?" she interrupts, her brown eyes widening with a not-so-distant memory. "We must've gone thousands of times. That's one of the things I've really missed over the last few months—going shopping with you."

Even though I'm not in the mood to try on clothes, a sentimental pang tugs at my heart. "Where are the dressing rooms?"

After an entire morning of intense shopping, I'm completely wiped out. The boutique is trashed, especially the dressing room that looks like a tornado touched down right in the middle of it. While Chloe has her purchases rung up at the front counter, Kirsten and I just stand in the middle of the mess, shaking our heads like stunned survivors of a natural disaster.

Frowning, I pick up a sage-green cocktail dress off the floor and put it back on its padded satin hanger, taking care to zip up the zipper and smooth out the wrinkles. I'm tempted to put the dress on one last time, even though I must've tried it on at least three dozen times during the course of our shopping marathon. The darn thing fits better than anything I've ever owned, which makes me mad at Chloe for making me try it on in the first place. I hate the feeling of wanting something I know I'll never have.

"Don't even think about it," Kirsten says, watching me hold the dress against my body.

"Are you kidding?" I answer as I stare at my reflection in the three-way mirror. "I'm totally broke. I don't even have enough money to put it on layaway."

"It was just a reality check—I want to make sure your best friend's clothing habit isn't rubbing off on you."

"It's been twelve years and it still hasn't happened yet," I tell her. "How about you? How are your finances holding up?"

The corners of Kirsten's mouth droop. "Not so good. Why do you think I was flirting with that ice-cream guy, anyway? I was starving."

Over Kirsten's shoulder I can see Chloe clearing out a good portion of the makeup counter. "I guess the ballet thing is taking off fast," I say in amazement. "Chloe's always been a spender, but I've never seen her throw cash around like this."

Kirsten's eyes glaze over as if she's lost in some distant thought. "It's weird, though, considering where she's living and everything."

"Weird? What's weird about it?"

"It's hard to explain," Kirsten answers.

Hard to explain? What on earth is she talking about? Double-checking to make sure Chloe is safely out of listening range, I nudge Kirsten in the ribs. "Tell me," I demand, my voice barely above a whisper. "What are you talking about?"

"Forget I said anything," Kirsten says, shaking her head. "I'm just shooting my mouth off."

If there's one thing I've figured out about Kirsten, it's that she's not the type of person who just talks for the sake of filling up dead air. Everything she says has a purpose. So there's absolutely no way I'm about to let this one slide. Normally I'd pounce all over her to get to the bottom of that comment she just made, but Chloe's waving at us to leave. I groan. I guess it'll have to wait until later.

On the way to her apartment, Chloe sits in the back seat and takes inventory of the new additions to her wardrobe. "In honor of your arrival, I got the both of you a little something."

Kirsten and I exchange stunned looks. "You didn't have to do that, Chloe, really," Kirsten says, looking majorly uncomfortable.

"It's just a little prezzie, no big deal." Pulling a flat box out of the bag, Chloe takes off the lid and produces a gorgeous, fiery red scarf, draping the cool silk over Kirsten's shoulder.

"Oooooh," Kirsten coos, looking instantly won over. She rubs the scarf against her face while trying to keep her eyes on the road. "This is so beautiful!"

Chloe beams proudly. "I thought you might like it. The color goes well with your black hair."

"I don't think you should give this to me," she says, halfheartedly.

"You have to take it," Chloe insists. "All sales are final. It says so on the tag."

There is no further argument from Kirsten.

Chloe reaches into the bag again and pulls out another box. This one is much larger than Kirsten's. "And for my dear friend, Miranda, in honor of our reunion."

Chloe drops the box in my lap, and even before I open it, I know what's inside. I can feel her eyes on me, waiting for me to lift the lid. "This is too much, Chloe," I tell her, the back of my neck breaking into a sweat.

"How can you say that? You haven't even looked inside," she argues playfully. "You might totally hate it!"

"Somehow I doubt that . . . " I open the box and push aside the tissue paper. Just as I suspected, the sage-green cocktail dress is lying there in the box with the price tag discreetly snipped, even though I remember that it cost nearly four hundred dollars.

Chloe tugs on one of my limp curls. "That's the one you liked, wasn't it?"

"Of course she liked it," Kirsten jumps in. "It took three saleswomen to pry it off her."

"It's so beautiful," I sigh with guilt.

Chloe beams, looking genuinely pleased with herself. "While you and Kirsten were waiting, I had them grab another dress from the stockroom—I wanted you to be surprised."

Oh, I'm surprised all right.

I find myself taking a quick mental inventory of

all the things in my backpack, trying to think of something I can give Chloe, but all I can come up with is a dirty sheetsàck and a used wad of tissues. Not exactly dream gift material.

"It's sweet of you, really, but it's much too extravagant," I say, delicately folding up the tissue paper and replacing the lid on the box. "You're already letting us stay at your place—you don't need to give us presents, too."

Kirsten takes the scarf off her shoulder and reluctantly hands it back to Chloe. "Miranda's right. This is way too much."

"All right, all right, look—I'm not dressing you guys up entirely out of the goodness of my heart. My motives are partially selfish," Chloe admits. "There's this huge cocktail party at the ballet director's house tomorrow night—he's invited all the students from the school who are applying to the apprenticeship program. It's going to be a really swank affair, and I'd really love for you guys to go with me—you know, for moral support."

I grab Chloe's hand and give it a squeeze. "Of course we'll be there."

"So you'll wear the dress?" she asks hopefully, squeezing me back.

"I guess I'll have to," I answer, smiling.

What was supposed to be a straight shot back to Chloe's place ends up being an extended loop as Chloe gives us a crash course in some of the sights of San Francisco. We cut through busy Chinatown and climb wealthy Nob Hill alongside a cable car, nearly burn out our brakes on the impossibly curvy Lombard Street, and stretch our legs in Ghirardelli Square, where Kirsten takes a picture of Chloe and me in front of the mermaid fountain. We then swing back toward North Beach and take an elevator to the top of Coit Tower, which sits atop the very steep Telegraph Hill and has the most magnificent view of the Bay.

Throughout our minitour, I've been noticing how much more laid-back people are here than they are back home on the East Coast. There's definitely a looser, more relaxed vibe out here that sort of melts all the little worries away. I imagine it would take a lot of work to be miserable in a city where the weather is nearly perfect and everywhere you turn there's a spectacular view.

Eventually we make our way over to the Haight, an edgy part of town once considered the promised land for hippies in the 1960s. A few remnants from that decade seem to still be hanging on, with their tie-dyes and dazed expressions. Time-warp victims aside, the neighborhood seems to have some cool vintage clothes and record stores, although I can't quite figure out why Chloe brought us here. It's not her style at all. It isn't until Kirsten parks the car in front of an old gray Victorian house that I start putting things together.

This is where Chloe lives.

"The place is enormous," I tell Chloe, helping her get some of the shopping bags out of the back seat. "Do you have a whole floor to yourself?"

"I wish," she answers ruefully. "I have to share it with nine other dancers and Madame Krakinov, one of the teachers. Talk about drama queens! And I thought *you* were bad, Miranda. Rooming with these girls is like living in the middle of a Broadway production—except intermission never comes."

"Come on." I laugh, looking at Kirsten for confirmation. "It can't be that bad!"

Kirsten shrugs and pinches her lips together. *No comment.*

We barely make it through the front door and already I can understand what she's talking about.

Two girls come flying down the staircase in the front hall, one screaming her guts out that she's going to kill the other for stealing her eyeliner. Kirsten and I press our backs against the front door while the girls tumble to the bottom of the stairs, attacking each other with a ferocity that makes TV wrestling look almost dignified.

"Maybe we should pull them apart," I offer, cringing as one of the girls starts crying hysterically, "or call 911."

"Don't worry—they're actually the best of friends. They do this every day," Chloe says, nearly yawning from boredom. "You know how sixteen-year-olds can get."

"Sure, I used to do this sort of thing all the time," Kirsten answers facetiously, looking completely horrified by the whole scene.

A door suddenly flies open at the end of the hall, and out comes an old woman with long gray hair, sunken cheeks, and black eyes that look like they could see through lead. Even from a distance, her presence is imposing. She sails down the hallway with frightening speed, grasping handfuls of her red, billowy skirt in each fist, her steps so smooth, it's as if she's on wheels. I don't even know the woman and *I* want to run for cover.

"Girls! Girls! That is enough!" the woman shouts, her gravelly voice punctuated by a clap of her wrinkled hands. "I will not have any more of this ludicrous behavior. We have guests!"

Both girls snap to attention and stop screaming. Under the watchful eye of the old woman, they help each other stand up and skulk away, seemingly disappointed that their game came to such an abrupt end.

When the girls are out of sight, the woman turns to me, a touch of mischief curling the corners of her mouth. "One of these days I'll let them keep going—maybe they'll do us all a favor."

"Madame Krakinov, this is Miranda," Chloe says, formally introducing us. "Miranda, this is Madame Krakinov."

Up close, Madame Krakinov is tiny and fragile, and not nearly as imposing as when she was flying down the hallway with her red skirt flowing behind her. Still, I get the impression that inside that small frame is a ferocious personality you wouldn't want to unleash.

"I see you've been enjoying a day of shopping." Madame casts a thin eyebrow in Chloe's direction. "Did you buy many beautiful things?"

"The bags aren't mine. Kirsten and Miranda wanted to do some shopping, so I showed them around," Chloe quickly says, looking down at the floor. "Miranda, show Madame the dress you bought."

The dress I bought? What is she talking about? Usually I have a big problem with being dragged into other people's lies, but the scared look on Chloe's face tells me to just go with it. Chloe's no

69

liar—she wouldn't be doing this unless she had a good reason.

I pull the green dress out of the bag and hold it up to my body. "It's the nicest dress I've ever owned," I say, which is actually the truth. "It was on sale."

Madame nods and reaches for the price tag. I find myself silently blessing the saleswoman for clipping it, even though I still know how much it cost. "Very pretty," Madame says finally, her tight lips pulling back across her face. I have the feeling this is as close as she gets to a smile. "Chloe, may I please speak with you privately?"

I don't dare look in Chloe's direction, but I swear I can almost hear the blood draining from her face.

"Sure," Chloe answers, her voice turning watery. She turns toward me and Kirsten, her eyes still focused on the floor. "Why don't you two go to my room—I'll be there in a second."

I have no idea what's about to happen, but I'm thinking that maybe Kirsten and I should stick around. Just in case.

"That's a good idea—she will join you upstairs," Madame says firmly. It's clear that we won't be sticking around. "It was nice meeting you, Miranda."

"Yeah," I answer in a vague voice, following Kirsten up the stairs, "it was nice meeting you, too."

What do you think that was all about?" I ask Kirsten, setting the shopping bags on the floor of Chloe's immaculately clean bedroom.

Kirsten plops down on Chloe's lace bedspread and kicks back, not bothering to take the extra step of removing her boots. Out of courtesy to Chloe, I take the lid off my dress box and slide it under Kirsten's feet.

"The old lady's creepy," Kirsten says, examining her short fingernails. "No wonder Chloe looked scared."

"But why should she be scared about telling her she went shopping? I don't get it."

"That's the way things work in the ballet world—they like to keep their dancers on a short leash," she says. "I had a friend who was in an apprenticeship program in New York. She said that the teachers ran their classes like military operations, and the pressure was so bad that dancers were having nervous breakdowns. She couldn't hack it and had to drop out."

I give Kirsten a skeptical frown. "Come on, it can't be that bad. . . ."

She shrugs at me. "Hey, that's what she told me. Maybe things are different here in California than they are in New York, but I doubt it if the other members of the dance faculty are anything like the *Madame*—"

Kirsten stops short and looks at the doorway. Chloe's standing there, her face looking ghostly pale against the vibrant pink of her dress.

"What happened?" I ask her.

"Nothing," Chloe answers. She's smiling, but I've known her long enough to see it's just for show—she's really rattled. "Madame wanted to make sure I was going to the party tomorrow night."

"And she couldn't say that in front of us?" I say.

"I don't know. She can be quirky sometimes." Chloe slips off her sandals and puts them in an empty shoe box in her closet, carefully enveloping them in a sheet of tissue paper. Striding across the wood floor in her bare feet, she points her toes and holds up her arms, turning a string of fierce pirouettes. She spins and spins, twirling at a dizzying speed, each movement rigid and exacting. I can feel her mood growing lighter with each turn, as though she's shedding whatever it was that happened with Madame.

"Did you see this?" Chloe asks me when she

finally comes to a precise stop. Daintily she picks up a blue picture frame with sea shells glued to the perimeter, a summer camp craft project I barely remember. "I found it when I moved out of the house."

I take one look and start laughing.

"Let me see!" Kirsten jumps off the bed and snatches the frame out of my hands. "Aw, look at you two—so cute! When was this taken?"

"Seventh grade," I answer, "on the day I got my braces. I was miserable when I came back from the orthodontist because my mouth tasted like I'd just eaten a frying pan. Chloe was cheering me up."

"So you had braces, too, Chloe?" Kirsten asks.

Chloe and I look at each other and bust out laughing.

"Mine were fake," she snickers. "I took two strips of aluminum foil and rolled them up. Then I molded the strips to the front of my teeth and *voilà*—fake braces. They tasted terrible and made my gums bleed, but it was worth it."

Kirsten gives Chloe this look like she's an absolute freak of nature. "And *why* did you do something like that?"

"She was being a good friend," I answer for her. "She didn't want me to suffer alone."

Chloe smiles modestly. "Miranda would've done the same for me. Besides, I was envious—she was getting all kinds of attention because of her braces."

73

"People called me metal mouth for weeks," I argue. "It was nothing to envy, I can assure you."

"Oh, come on—you enjoyed every minute of it. . . ."

While I explain to Chloe why she's totally wrong, Kirsten just stands there, smirking at us. I stop midsentence and look at her. "What's so funny?" I ask.

"I was just thinking how cool it is that you've guys have been friends so long, you can argue about what happened in seventh grade," Kirsten answers.

"You should see us when we compare our versions of *first* grade," Chloe says. "It can get pretty ugly."

"But what I mean is, it's great that you guys have been able to stay friends for so long. My mom and I moved around so much when I was a kid that I don't think I've been friends with any one person for maybe more than two years or so," Kirsten says. "I can't even imagine what's it's like to know someone so well and to have them know *me*."

"I'm just the opposite," Chloe says. "I can't imagine what it's like *not* to be so close to someone. Luckily, I won't have to because I'm pretty sure Miranda and I will always be friends, right Miranda?"

"Of course," I answer. "I can't imagine why not."

One picture leads to another, and the next thing I know, Chloe's hauling out photo albums and yearbooks, reconstructing our friendship from our first day of school together all the way to graduation. I was afraid our trip down memory lane would be a giant snore-fest for Kirsten, but she can't seem to get enough of our stories. And I can't get enough of hearing Chloe's version of our shared history, which is often not even close to what I remember. How can two people who lived through the same events have such different memories of what happened?

All this nostalgia leaves us pretty hungry, so we head down to the kitchen for some grub. On the way downstairs, we pass a group of dancers practicing a jazz routine in the parlor for fun, and a few more serious students using the staircase banister as a barre for their warm-ups. Even though the place is crawling with people, no one's in the kitchen, and as you probably suspected, the refrigerator isn't exactly overflowing with tasty stuff.

The best Chloe can come up with is a few reheated plates of leftover tofu, brown rice, and steamed broccoli. I think I'm going to gag.

After we choke down our dinners, Chloe whips out all the different face creams and masks she bought today, and we slather our faces with the expensive goop. She's got everything from aromatherapy mud masks to a deep conditioner for your cuticles. I haven't quite figured out why the pricey stuff is supposed to be better than the cheap stuff, but what do I care? It's Chloe's money.

With the big party tomorrow and an upcoming audition, Chloe decides to turn in early, while Kirsten and I take our scrubbed faces and growling stomachs out for some *real* food. On a previous trip to the city, Kirsten remembers this great *taqueria* in a Latino neighborhood called The Mission, so we head over to that part of town to see if it's still around. Luckily, it is.

We grab a seat by the window of the dingy little restaurant and watch people stroll by, enjoying the balmy night air. It's been such a long day that I feel my body moving beyond tired to the point where I'm hyper. I'm running on pure adrenaline now.

Kirsten scans her laminated menu, splotched with dried-up hot sauce. "I never thought a four-dollar burrito would look expensive to me," she says, frowning ruefully.

"I know what you mean," I tell her. "My money's almost gone—the train trip really wiped me out. I don't have enough to keep myself fed, let alone move on to the next place. I'm going to have to get a job."

Kirsten rolls her eyes to the ceiling. "Oh, no, she said the 'j' word."

"Do you have any better ideas? How are we supposed to get money?"

"I don't know." She shrugs. "We could rob banks, sell our blood, gather scrap metal—anything but get a lousy job."

I reach for my water and catch a glint of my silver rope ring reflecting a bit of low light from the wall lamp. While Kirsten keeps on talking about alternative ways to get cash in our pockets, I suddenly feel distant, as if I'm sinking to the bottom of a cold, deep swimming pool. Everything takes on a blue tinge, and sounds are muffled beyond recognition. Movements happen so slowly, it feels like it takes years for me to blink.

"Let's get out of here," I interrupt, the words streaming out slow and bubbly. A thin trail of beads form on my upper lip. Kirsten's face seems to turn an eerie shade of blueberry.

"What's the deal?" Kirsten complains, chomping on a tortilla chip. "We haven't even ordered yet—"

"I don't feel so good . . ." A queasy wave breaks over me as I stand up, gripping the edge of the sticky wooden table to steady myself. Without any further explanation, I head straight for the door.

Kirsten follows close behind, and when we

finally make it outside, she grabs me by the elbow. "What's going on?"

I suck in a deep breath of the cool night air, the fresh influx of oxygen clearing away some of the bubbles in my head. "I didn't get any sleep last night. And so much has happened to me in the last two days. I just looked at the ring Dustin gave me and . . . oh, never mind—it's stupid."

Kirsten leads me over to a nearby bench and gives me the rest of her soda. I try to take a sip, but it just won't go down.

"It made you miss him, right?" she says.

"There's this big, empty hole in the middle of my chest," I tell her. "It feels like it's never going to go away."

"I wish I could tell you the hurt will go away soon, but I'd be lying. It's just something you have to get through."

Nearby, a few kids with skateboards tip an empty garbage can on its side and take turns jumping over it. "I'm not even sure I want to stop hurting, you know, because that would mean that I didn't love him anymore," I say.

Sipping her soda, Kirsten stares out into space as if she's thinking over what I've just said. "Not necessarily. I mean, of course you're going to miss him and you're going to feel like a piece of you is gone, but you don't have to be depressed and hurt to prove that you love Dustin. Love doesn't work that way."

I didn't want to cry, but already I can feel the tears welling up in my eyes. "I don't see how I can help it . . ."

"All you have to do is decide that you're going to be happy, that you're going to enjoy your visit with Chloe, and you're not going to let the separation from Dustin get you down."

"Is that what you usually do when you have a breakup?"

"It depends," Kirsten says. "If the guy was a jerk—no problem, good riddance. But if it was someone I liked, I usually punch my fist into the wall, then stay in my pj's and watch TV for a week straight. After that, I'm usually ready to dip my toes back in the dating pool again. My technique for broken heart recovery won't work for you, though. You're a different animal altogether."

Taking Kirsten's soda from her, I make another attempt at drinking. This time, I'm able to choke down a little of it. "When I was on the train, Mike told me that it didn't have to be over with Dustin if I didn't want it to. He said we could have a long-distance relationship."

Kirsten's slate eyes squint at me skeptically. "I hate to say it, but they rarely work."

"That's not what *he* said," I answer, my face reddening.

"Hey, don't get mad. I'm just telling you what I know."

I cross my arms in front of my chest. "You don't

know what's going to happen. It *can* work out. I've seen it."

"I'm sure it can. But you have to be realistic about the possibility that you and Dustin might grow apart," Kirsten says. "And I'm not necessarily talking about Dustin finding someone new. *You* might be the one who falls for someone else."

The burning heat crawls all the way up to my eyebrows. "That's not going to happen," I answer with a conviction that surprises even myself.

Kirsten blinks hard a few times, obviously caught off guard. "Hey, I didn't mean anything by it. I was just talking . . . "

"That's fine," I say, standing up. "But I don't feel like talking anymore."

It isn't until almost noon the next day that I wake up from a dead sleep to find Kirsten and Chloe long gone. Kirsten's blankets and sheets are on the floor in a chaotic ball, right where she'd been sleeping, while Chloe's bed is neatly made, wrinkles smoothed out to perfection. She's left a note for me there on pretty butterfly paper with her name embossed in gold, saying she's gone to class for the afternoon and for me to help myself to food downstairs in the kitchen. The note also reminds me about the party tonight. I'm to meet her back here at five to get ready.

I put on a pair of sweats and twist my hair into a bun using one of Chloe's pencils to hold it in place, so I can look at least somewhat presentable to the rest of the residents. It hardly matters, as I soon find out, because the house is totally empty—or at least I'm guessing it is because I can't hear music or thumping feet coming from any of the rooms. I stumble down the staircase, past the silent, narrow hallway that leads to

Madame Krakinov's apartment, down into the dark kitchen that sinks just below street level, keeping my fingers crossed that I'll be able to find something to eat that didn't come from a health food store.

After a thorough search of the cupboards, the best thing I can come up with is a stale box of organic cornflakes and no milk, so I reach in and eat it dry right out of the box. *It bites not having any money,* I think to myself as I choke down the sawdust flakes, thinking back to all the times along the way when I should've been more careful with my cash. Like all those restaurants Kirsten and I ate in when we should've been buying stuff at supermarkets. Or the nights we checked into hotels when we should've tried to stick it out in the car. If only we'd done that at least a third of the time, I'd have a decent amount of money to get by on right now. Who knew I'd rip through my savings so fast?

"I see you've found something to eat," a gravelly voice calls from behind me. I whip around and see the tiny shadowy outline of Madame Krakinov in the doorway. She clicks on the overhead fluorescent lights, practically blinding me.

"Yeah." I freeze while Madame's disapproving eyes take in the sight of my arm shoved deep into the box, all the way up to the elbow. I pull my hand out, along with a shower of cornflakes that fall like confetti on the floor. "Sorry . . ."

"There's a dustpan and broom in the closet behind you," she says. "I trust you've learned how to use both."

"Yes, Madame," I hear myself saying as I scurry over to the closet to pick up the mess. I hardly know the woman at all, but I find myself having this overwhelming need to please her and I'm not exactly sure why. There's something in her personality that conveys a sense of disapproval with the world and it makes you want to take on the challenge of being the one person who can get her to smile. Looking at the mess of cornflakes on the floor, I'm pretty certain that person isn't going to be me.

Madame glides over to the big round kitchen table, her stick of a body rising out of a massive paisley skirt. She takes a seat, and the skirt gently floats down around her like dust settling back to earth after a tornado. She watches me closely until every last crumb has been picked up.

"Come, sit down here." Madame pats the chair beside her, her wrinkly lips stretched tightly over her teeth.

I take a seat, hands folded tightly, pressed between my knees. My heart nervously flutters in my rib cage while I wait for Madame to say something. She closes her eyes as if she's listening to distant music or conjuring ancient spirits, her breathing becoming so light and still that I start to wonder if she's slipped out of consciousness. Just when I nearly reach for the phone to call an ambulance, she opens her eyes again. "So you and Chloe have known each other since childhood?" she asks me.

"We've been best friends since first grade," I answer, my voice wavering.

Madame nods. "That's nice. Very special," she says. "And you've come to visit with her for a few days?"

"Yes, Madame—well, no . . . we are visiting, but we don't know for how long."

"Four days, five days, a week?"

"We really don't know."

Madame lays a bony hand on the tabletop, her skin so pale, I can almost see right through it. "I admire the young people today—they go about their business without a care in the world. They do whatever they feel like whenever they feel like it. When I was young, we had all these rules of etiquette to worry about—we were always concerned about what was polite and proper. You young people are very lucky to be so free and happy all the time."

Although Madame's tone of voice is light, there's no mistaking the hard-edged point she's trying to get across. "I didn't realize Kirsten and I weren't welcome here," I say.

"Of course you are welcome here," she says, "but you must realize that this is not a hotel. This is a house for serious young women who are training to be dancers. It is important that my girls have as little outside distraction as possible. The focus should be on dancing at all times."

"I understand that, but I didn't know any of this before I got here. Chloe said we could stay, so I figured—"

"Chloe is constantly distracted. Her mind is on everything *but* dance." Anger flashes behind Madame's black eyes. "When I first saw her I thought that she had the potential to go further than any of my students ever had before, but I'm starting to have my doubts now. Her thoughts are not where they should be."

I swallow hard. "Chloe's that good, huh?"

Madame's eyes narrow. "You don't know that? How can you be best friends and not know that?"

"I've always thought she was really good," I answer in my own defense, "but I don't know enough about dance to tell *how* good."

"You don't have to know dance—you can just feel it, *in here*." She thumps her heart with her fist.

To some degree, I understand what Madame is saying. Looking back, I know that Chloe's performances always leave me feeling breathless. There's so much joy in her movement, so much grace in the slightest tilt of her head and the bend of her wrist. As far as I've been concerned, Chloe always radiates a magnetic light onstage that outshines all those other poor saps who have the misfortune of being next to her, but I've figured I was biased because I was her best friend. I guess I was wrong.

"It is important at this stage that Chloe surround herself only with people who support her talent," Madame says in an accusing tone.

"I *am* supportive!"

Madame glares at me. "There is no need, Miranda, to raise your voice."

"I'm sorry," I say softly. "But I don't think you're being very fair."

"To whom? You or Chloe?"

"To either of us," I argue. "I don't think you're giving Chloe enough credit—for as long as I've known her, she's lived and breathed ballet. She's never had a problem balancing her personal life and dance. And as for me, you don't know anything about who I am, so how can you say I'm not a supportive friend?"

Clutching a fistful of skirt in each hand, Madame glares at me. "Perhaps you've misunderstood. In my mind, if you are not a dancer yourself, then you are merely a distraction. If you speak of anything that does not involve dance, you are ruining Chloe's concentration. She has a very important audition coming up soon—one that could have a tremendous impact on her entire career. If you are a true friend, you will give her the support she needs by leaving."

"Madame, we just got here," I plead. "Kirsten and I have nowhere to go."

"I will give you three days," she says, glaring at me. "No more—understand?"

We're in big trouble," I tell Kirsten the second she walks through Chloe's door. "Madame Krakinov is kicking us out."

The smile fades from Kirsten's face as she closes the door behind her. "What?"

I pace back and forth across the hardwood floor, my nails bitten down to my fingertips. "She cornered me when I was having breakfast. She said that Chloe needs to focus on her dancing and we're just distracting her."

"What a witch!" Kirsten shouts loud enough for her voice to carry out into the hallway. "I can't believe she's doing this to us."

"Well, believe it—we have three days to get out."

"Where are we supposed to go?"

I shrug. "I've been trying to figure that out for the last few hours. I called a few youth hostels, but they're booked solid this time of year. Hotels are so expensive—I don't even have enough money for one night."

"And you know *I* don't," Kirsten says, shaking

her head in disbelief. "I can't believe she's doing this to us."

I plop down on Chloe's bed, my head feeling as though it's stuffed with cotton. I'd love nothing better than to crawl under the covers and make the whole world disappear. "I guess the only thing we can do is find a job."

"Don't talk crazy," she says. "There has to be something else we can do. Does Chloe have a phone in here?"

"She has a cell phone, but I think she took it with her. Why?"

"Have you tried calling your parents?"

"To ask them for money?" I start laughing. "Like *that*'s going to happen."

Kirsten sits beside me on the bed. "Come on, you've got great parents. You know they'd help you out. All you have to do is ask."

I shake my head furiously. "My mom and dad never forget anything. I can see it now—I'll be forty, with a family of my own, sitting around the table at Thanksgiving, and Dad will try to liven up the conversation by telling for the hundredth time the story of how they bailed out poor Miranda when she foolishly ran out of money in San Francisco. No, thank you—I'm going to figure this one out on my own."

Kirsten chews thoughtfully on her lower lip. "What about your brother?" she asks.

"Even worse," I tell her. "No dice."

Diving into her pack, Kirsten grabs a handful of quarters. "Tell you what—*I'll* call *my* mom. I have no pride."

You've certainly proved that before, I think wryly to myself as I follow Kirsten down the stairs and outside to the corner pay phone. I can picture Kirsten's mom, Caroline, in the library of her quaint New Jersey bed-and-breakfast, taking tea with her guests, hardly suspecting that she's about to get a call from the daughter, who only contacts her when she needs something. If I were Caroline, I'd hang up as soon as I heard Kirsten's voice.

Kirsten punches the number on the keypad and leans against the booth. The curved edges of her face harden, and her eyes turn cold. She's ready for a showdown. "Yeah, put Caroline on," she barks into the receiver. "It's her daughter."

I cross my fingers behind my back, hoping we've at least caught Caroline in a good mood. Regardless of how Kirsten feels, Caroline's been really good to us, and I hate to take advantage of her kindness any more than we already have. But at this point, she's our only hope.

"Hi, it's me," she says. "How's it going? We made it to San Francisco, finally . . . the weather's been pretty nice . . . "

Kirsten's never been one for small talk. I'm impressed that she's actually making an effort. I guess she realizes the seriousness of the situation.

"Miranda's here." Kirsten shoves the receiver in my face. "Say something to my mom."

Flustered, I take the phone. "Hi, Caroline."

"How are you, dear?" Caroline says. In my mind's eye I can see her soft, round face smiling at me. "Is everything all right?"

"Everything's fine," I answer as I watch Kirsten feeding the pay phone with quarters. "How are you?"

"Caught off guard," she answers. "My daughter wants something, doesn't she?"

The air catches in my throat. What should I say? I don't want to blow Kirsten's setup, but what good would it do to lie? Caroline's no fool—she knows what's going on here.

"Yeah," I answer timidly. "Sorry about that."

"What are you sorry for?"

"I don't know," I confess. "Guilt by association."

A suspicious look creeps across Kirsten's face. She snatches the phone back from me. "I'm almost out of change, so I'll make this quick. Miranda and I need some money."

Pause.

"It's a long story," she continues. "Basically, my wallet got stolen, and the hotels around here are incredibly expensive. We've been sleeping out on the street the last few nights. I didn't want to bug you, but this scary guy almost attacked Miranda last night, and she's terrified of spending another night out here."

My chin drops. "What are you doing?" I whisper. "Don't make up stuff!"

Kirsten covers the receiver with her hand and gives me a look to shut up. "A couple hundred dollars," she says. "Uh-huh . . . uh-huh . . . okay . . . bye." She hangs up.

"So what happened?" I ask, still mad she dragged me into her lie.

"She didn't buy it." Kirsten sighs. "She told me to call back when I had a better story."

"Why didn't you just tell her the truth?"

"It's too complicated to explain in thirty seconds. It didn't seem urgent enough—I had to dress it up a little."

I grit my teeth. "In three days, we'll have no money and nowhere to go," I tell her. "Is that urgent enough for you?"

Kirsten backs away. "Hey, don't get mad at me. At least *I* tried to get some money. I still have a few quarters left if you want to call your mom."

"I told you, that's not happening."

"Fine, it's not happening," Kirsten says. "So what are we supposed to do now?"

"Give me your change," I say, holding out my hand. Kirsten drops the quarters in my palm. "Let's go get a newspaper."

Why aren't you two getting ready?" Chloe asks as soon as she walks in the door.

Kirsten and I look up from the *San Francisco Chronicle* want ads we've been poring over for the last hour or so. Chloe reads the look of dismay on our faces and matches our expressions with one of her own.

"What's wrong?" Chloe asks.

"Madame asked us to leave," I answer heavily. "She doesn't want us hanging around."

Chloe strides over to her closet and pulls out my new green dress along with two others. "Who cares what she says? This is my room. You can stay here as long as you want."

"I don't think you understand," I tell her. "She's kicking us out."

"Yeah, right. Look, the woman says a lot of things—she's old." Chloe pulls a pair of conservative black pumps out of her closet. "How do you think these would look with my little black dress?"

Kirsten looks at me. "Maybe you're just overreacting to what she said."

"I'm not overreacting!" I shout, painfully aware of the irony. "This is serious, guys. I'm telling you that she wants us out."

Chloe drops her shoes and takes a seat beside me on the floor. "It's not that we don't believe you. It's just that sometimes you can be a little, well, *sensitive*," she says. "You have a tendency to misread what people are saying and blow them out of proportion."

"You're telling *me*," Kirsten chimes in.

"Are you sure you're not just reading into something she said?" Chloe says.

I'm so ticked off right now, I'd like to throttle them both. "Look, guys, there was no misreading this, okay?" I answer in my own defense. "Madame was loud and clear: We have to get out—in three days."

Chloe pats my arm in a patronizing way that makes my blood boil. "Madame is senile—she says a lot of wacky things."

"She seemed perfectly sane to me," I argue.

"I'm sure she did," Chloe says. "But it doesn't matter what she says, because I'm really close to the director of the school, Dr. Friel—the one whose house we're going to tonight—and he'll let you stay here if I ask him. It isn't a problem."

Kirsten crumples up her section of the want ads and tosses it into the wastebasket. "Well that was a complete waste of an afternoon. Hit the panic button a little prematurely, don't you think, Miranda?"

I sigh loudly. "Okay, so what if we do stay? We still don't have any money."

"I'm not worried," Kirsten answers. "Something will come along."

Or someone . . . like a guy you can sponge off of. . . .

Chloe floats to her feet. "Let's not worry about this stuff tonight—we have a party to get ready for," she says. "Kirsten, you can wear my navy sheath if you want—I think it'd look great with your new scarf."

While Chloe plays fashion consultant to Kirsten, I just sit there on the floor, stewing in my own juices. Suddenly I'm not in much of a party mood.

"Stop being such a sourpuss, Miranda," Chloe says, reading my mind. "You're going to have an awesome time. I can't wait to show off my old high school pal to everyone. Hurry up and get that dress on so I can do your hair. . . ."

Just to be stubborn, I wait a full thirty seconds before I put down the newspaper and pick up the dress.

Chloe doesn't stop talking about the party from the moment we start getting ready to the second we step off the California cable car at the top of Nob Hill. The whole time she keeps saying how extravagant it's going to be, and how lucky we are to be going, and how glad she is that we'll be there to keep her from feeling awkward. She builds it up so much that I'm completely convinced there's no way the occasion could possibly live up to the hype. I was wrong.

It all begins with the house. Or should I say, *mansion*. Painted a soft rose, the stunning Victorian building sits primly on the hill, just reeking of history and old money. In the deepening blue of the evening sky, I stand on the front walkway, frozen by the warm glow of light that pours from each one of the magnificent windows.

Chloe loops her arm through mine. "Are you going to stand out here all night, or can we go inside?"

"Sorry," I answer numbly. "It's so beautiful."

"Wait until you see the inside," Chloe says. "You'll just die."

Kirsten joins me on the other side, and the three of us walk arm in arm up the brick walkway to the massive front door. Dressed to the nines and cranking up the attitude, we're a wall of cool confidence. On our own, we probably wouldn't have enough self-assurance to get by in a room of incredibly wealthy, well-connected social climbers. But together, we're fierce.

"Buddy system tonight, right?" Chloe asks. That's the phrase we use to make sure we stay in close proximity to one another when a social situation is too intimidating. Buddy system rules require that you never leave your friend's side unless they say it's okay, and you absolutely never leave the party without them.

"It's definitely a buddy night," I answer as Kirsten rings the doorbell.

Chloe's breathing is shallow and nervous. "How do I look?" She turns to me and smooths down her dress.

"Fabulous," I tell her, my eyes scanning her simple black dress, thin strand of delicate pearls, and low pumps. "Very elegant."

"I wanted to go conservative, you know," she says. "It's always best to play it safe at these kinds of parties. You look great too, by the way."

"Thanks," I answer, feeling myself blushing

already. I wonder how much a red face clashes with a green dress.

"Sounds like you guys have a mutual admiration society going on over there," Kirsten says, playing with the ends of the new scarf she tied around her neck.

"Are you feeling left out?" I ask.

"No, I'm feeling nauseous," Kirsten jokes.

The front door opens, and a butler in a tuxedo appears in the doorway. "Good evening, ladies," he says. "Please come in."

Chloe leads the way, and we fall in behind her, entering the grand foyer. The floor is covered in smooth marble tiles that gleam like mirrors, and the crystal chandelier above sends shards of light raining down on an enormous vase filled with exotic flowers in various shades of orange and purple. The opulence reminds me a bit of Jay's girlfriend's house in Virginia, but instead of exuding warm southern charm, this place has a cool, city sophistication. It's gorgeous.

"May I get you anything?" the butler asks.

"No, thank you," Chloe answers in a startlingly calm, clear voice. Her jitters seem to have evaporated into thin air. "We're fine for now."

He points to the staircase straight ahead. "You may go right up to the parlor, if you wish."

Chloe nods and strides over to it with confident grace, while Kirsten and I hold on to one another to keep from tripping on the slippery floor in our high heels. Chloe leads the way up the stairs while we giggle and try to keep our balance, like Cinderella being followed by her two klutzy stepsisters.

Kirsten leans toward me. "I wouldn't mind living in this dump," she whispers.

"Me either," I whisper back.

The sound of piano music grows louder as we reach the top of the stairs. The music is so fluid and perfect, I thought it was being piped in by some hidden stereo, until I spot the sleek black grand piano in the corner of the room and the distinguished-looking pianist sitting behind it.

"That guy's playing Carnegie Hall next week with the New York Philharmonic," she says.

"No way," I answer, trying not to look awestruck.

Chloe nods. "Dr. Friel knows tons of important people. Keep your eyes peeled. There're probably a few other celebrities floating around."

I try to look for some famous faces, but my senses are too overwhelmed by the whole scene to take it all in. Couches and chairs in a luxurious ruby velvet are clustered in small groupings throughout the room, in between tables dressed with delicate white linens that are loaded with tropical fruits and imported cheeses. Waiters silently make the rounds, carrying elegant appetizers on silver trays. Men and women dressed as if they were ready for a night out at the opera engage in civilized conversation. Sprinkled among the refined guests are a few of the dancers from Chloe's school, huddled together for moral support, looking slightly unnerved and out of place in such an extravagant setting.

As usual, even this scene isn't too intimidating for Kirsten, who dives right into the party without a second thought, chasing after a darkly handsome waiter carrying a tray of lobster canapés. I'm left shrinking behind Chloe, my hands damp and cold.

"Do you go to a lot of parties like this?" I ask.

"Every chance I get." Chloe cranes her long neck as if she's looking for someone. "You have to work it. You know what I mean?"

Not really, I think to myself.

A tall, blond waiter with sexy dimples turns the corner and nudges a silver tray under my nose. "Would you like one?" he asks me.

Taken aback by the sudden offering, I stare down at the tray. "What are those things?"

Those things? Way to sound sophisticated, Miranda, chides a voice in the back of my brain. *He'll never guess that this is your first elegant cocktail party.*

"They're baby potatoes filled with crème fraîche and Osetra caviar." The waiter gives me a coy grin. "Try one—I bet you'll love it."

"Why not?" I say, feeling a bit flush. I try to pick up one of the appetizers as delicately as possible, but my fingers feel thick and unruly next to the itty-bitty potatoes.

"That's a beautiful dress, by the way," he says, at the very same moment I pop the potato in my mouth.

"Thanks." The salty fish eggs burst on my tongue, leaving behind a pretty heinous aftertaste. If I were alone in this room, I'd probably run over to one of those huge flowerpots and spit the caviar into it, but since I'm standing in a crowded room with a devastatingly handsome waiter looking at me, I'll just swallow it instead. *Yuck*.

"That was lovely," I tell him, trying to look cosmopolitan.

The waiter nudges the tray toward me. "Have another."

"I couldn't possibly—"

"No, go ahead," he insists. "This crowd doesn't seem to be eating very much. Whatever doesn't get eaten will get thrown away."

I want to protest, but the pleading look on his gorgeous face is impossible to resist. I reach for another potato.

The waiter smiles. "I guess I'll see you around later," he says with a wink.

"Yeah . . . later . . . " I smile back.

When he's gone, I discreetly hide the potato behind a silver candelabra on the fireplace mantel.

Chloe raises her eyebrows at me. "Are you done?"

"Done what?" I ask.

"Flirting."

My breath catches in my throat. "I was *not* flirting. He was giving me potatoes."

"Whatever . . . "

"No, really—I wasn't flirting," I insist.

Chloe shrugs. "Fine, you weren't flirting. Come along, there's lots to do."

"Where are we going?"

She takes me by the arm and pulls me deep into the crowd. "There's someone I want you to meet."

Dr. Friel, this is Miranda Burke, my oldest and dearest friend," Chloe says, thrusting me in the center of a tight circle of people who look like serious contenders for the Nobel prize. "Miranda, I'd like you to meet Dr. Friel, the director of our school."

Dr. Friel looks nothing like I'd imagined in my mind's eye: Somehow I was thinking of someone older and much more decrepit, like Madame—and yet now that he's standing right in front of me, he looks exactly like the kind of person who would live in an elegant place like this. Tall and broad-shouldered yet slender, Dr. Friel is a handsome, middle-aged gentleman with a long mustache and a slightly receding hairline that has just the right salt-and-pepper mix, and a generous demeanor. His expensive-looking tuxedo I'm sure has seen many parties such as this one, yet I can imagine him looking forward to the moment when the last guest will leave so he can slip into his silk smoking jacket and sip cognac by the fire. . . . Or maybe

I've seen way too many James Bond flicks, and my imagination is getting the best of me.

Dr. Friel offers me his hand. On the way to extending mine, I brush my palm against the side of my dress to soak up any excess moisture. "It's nice to meet you," I tell him. His handshake is whisper light. "You have a lovely home."

"Thank you very much, my dear," Dr. Friel says. While he speaks, the circle of people move in slightly and cock their ears, as though they are hanging on to his every word. "It's a pleasure to have you here."

I feel pressure to say something, so I fall back on an old small-talk standby. "Chloe's told me a lot about you."

"You can't believe everything you hear," he says, playing with the ends of his mustache. "Unless it's good, of course."

It's hardly an original line, yet everyone in the circle starts laughing as though they've never heard anything so witty in their entire lives. A few feet away I notice Madame Krakinov standing by, wearing a frothy ballerina skirt as blue as the sky over her same old black leotard. With her arms crossed tightly in front of her and her lips pinched together, Madame's the only one who's not laughing.

Dr. Friel casts a stern but gentle eye in Chloe's direction. "So are you ready for the big audition on Monday?"

"Of course," Chloe answers with a level of

confidence that could be mistaken for arrogance. "I was ready the day they announced it."

Dr. Friel responds with a deep, round laugh, which his lackeys soon imitate. "Chloe's our little diva-in-the-making. You know your friend is going to be a star, don't you, Miranda?"

Chloe beams, lapping up the praise like a puppy.

"I've heard that," I answer, glancing in Madame's direction. Her lips are pressed so tightly together, the edges have turned white. If I didn't know any better, I'd think that she was jealous of Chloe.

"Thanks for the noncompliment," Chloe says, nudging me jokingly in the ribs.

I can feel the stares of the other party goers stinging my cheeks. "We all know you're wonderful, Chloe. It's my job to keep your head from swelling."

"There's no such thing as a swollen head when you're as talented as Chloe," Dr. Friel corrects me. "There's only confidence in your ability. We should all be lucky to have such confidence."

Chloe flashes me a brilliant smile. "Hear that? You should be nicer to me—I'm going to be famous."

"When you're a big star, will you still remember me—you know, one of the little people?" I ask.

"I'll give you tickets to all my performances," Chloe says. "We'll vacation in Italy together."

Dr. Friel pats Chloe on the shoulder like a proud father and looks at me. "So, Miranda, what is your field of study?"

"She's extremely intelligent," Chloe jumps in, attempting to save me from certain embarrassment, "and she loves to read."

"Both very useful qualities," Dr. Friel says, amused wrinkles radiating from the corners of his eyes. "She'd probably make an excellent personal assistant for you, Chloe, when you go on tour."

Chloe's eyes light up. "Oh! Wouldn't that be great, Miranda? You could help me run errands and answer all my phone calls—we could spend all of our free time together!"

Dr. Friel seems pleased that his idea has excited his student so much. I really want to tell Chloe that although I love her like a sister, I have higher aspirations for my life than taking messages and making trips to the bank to cash her diva-sized checks, but the pressure of a lighthearted social situation calls for a different answer.

"That sounds like a lot of fun," I say, drumming up as much enthusiasm as the crowd seems to require.

Out of the corner of my eye, I see Madame shaking her head and walking away.

So much for the buddy system," I mention to Kirsten when I meet her at the cheese table after being gradually squeezed out of the social circle by Dr. Friel's admirers. I waited on the fringes for quite a long time, keeping close to Chloe like I'd promised, but after a while she seemed to forget I was standing nearby. It doesn't matter to me, as long as she's comfortable—and she looked more than comfortable. She was basking in the spotlight.

"It looks like Chloe's already got a following," Kirsten says.

"Yeah, they really love her—except for Madame," I whisper confidentially. "I'm pretty sure she's jealous."

Kirsten grabs a buffet plate. "Well, that goes without saying. An old crab like that—of course she'd be jealous of someone younger and more beautiful who is probably going to have a more successful career than she ever had. If I were Chloe, I'd watch my back." She loads a big slab of brie on her plate along with a pile of strawberries. "Would you look at all this food? No one's hardly touched a thing! I swear these people don't eat at all. Why cater the stupid party if you're not going to eat?"

"Maybe having food around gives them the illusion that they're having a good time," I answer.

Kirsten flags down a waiter carrying a tray of shrimp. "Hey, you—come over here." It's the same gorgeous one with the dimples who brought me the caviar earlier. The waiter follows as Kirsten coaxes him into a secluded corner behind a potted palm tree. "No one eats this stuff, do they?"

"Not really," he answers.

"I didn't think so," Kirsten says. She steals a quick glance between the palm fronds, then unties the scarf from around her neck.

I can feel my eyes bulging out of my head. "What are you doing?"

Kirsten holds the ends of the scarf in both hands and has the waiter tip the tray into her makeshift pouch.

"You're stealing shrimp?" I say, keeping an eye out to make sure no one else is witnessing this unbelievable event.

"Hey, if no one else is going to eat it . . . " Kirsten shakes her scarf pouch to make room for the rest. She looks at the waiter. "Tilt the tray down just a little more."

The waiter smiles at me while he obliges. "Are you having a good time?"

"Well, the evening has certainly taken an interesting turn," I say dryly. Remembering what Chloe said earlier about me flirting, I try to seem serious and a little bit detached, but it's almost impossible not to smile back.

He looks around, then leans in toward me like he's about to whisper a secret. "Everyone seems to take themselves so seriously, don't you think? But you seem like a nice girl."

"I am," I say, blushing deeply. "I mean, I can be."

"I knew it, I can tell."

I give him a sly grin. "How can you tell?"

The waiter pouts his lips and shrugs. "It's just a feeling I get."

Kirsten slides the last shrimp into her pouch, then ties the top in such a way that it makes a handle. When she's finished, she ends up with something that resembles a small evening bag. A bag full of shrimp, that is.

"I have to get back to work," the waiter says. He reaches into the inside pocket of his tuxedo jacket and pulls out a business card. "You know, I'm a pretty nice guy, too. Why don't you call me and we can go out sometime?"

Stunned, I take the card from him. "Thanks," I answer, looking down at it. TOP-NOTCH CATERERS, INC.—WHEN ELEGANCE IS THE ONLY OPTION . . .

"It's the company's card, but if you call the number, you should be able to get ahold of me, no problem," he says. "My name is Spencer."

"Right," I murmur, looking at the card. "Thank you, Spencer."

"I'd better get back to work," he says. "I didn't catch your name, though."

"Miranda."

"I hope to hear from you, Miranda," Spencer says before walking away.

"She shoots, she scores!" Kirsten teases, reaching into her scarf for a shrimp. "Let's go to the kitchen and make out with the waiters for food."

I curl my lip in disgust. "I'm not that desperate. Besides, I have a boyfriend."

"Could have fooled me."

"We were just talking," I answer in my own defense. "I wasn't trying to lead him on—"

"I know, I know," Kirsten interrupts, "he was nice, and you didn't want to be rude. It's the same old line every girlfriend uses to convince herself that she's being good. I bet when you were talking to Spencer, Dustin didn't even cross your mind once."

"Sure, he did. I mean, he must've . . . " My shoulders slump. I'm suddenly overcome with guilt. "Does this mean I'm a bad girlfriend?"

Kirsten smiles gently. "It means you're normal. I'm just razzing you, Miranda. A little harmless flirting never hurt anyone."

My body temperature feels like it just jumped ten degrees. "It *was* harmless enough," I stammer, reaching for a cool glass of sparkling water from one of the passing waiters, "but when I think of Dustin doing the same thing—it doesn't seem so harmless."

"Look, if you want to be able to be friendly to other guys, you're just going to have to give Dustin the same freedom," Kirsten says. "If you don't, you'll push him away."

I frown ruefully, thinking of Dustin somewhere in London right now. "It's not like he could get any farther away."

It's nearly one in the morning and more than half of the party goers have made their exit. Kirsten and I have retired to one of the red velvet couches in front of the fireplace, watching Chloe work the room like a politician while waiters thrust tray after tray of untouched food in our faces. I'm stuffed to the gills, and my feet are tired. I'm ready to go home.

Unfortunately for us, Chloe seems far from done. It's amazing to watch her from a distance, looking so poised and elegant—she hardly seems like the same person I used to have spitting contests with in our backyard. In fact, she hardly seems like the same person I graduated from high school with only a few months ago. Chloe always had everything going for her, but we were just high school kids—there was no way of knowing how far she could go. And now, just three months later, everyone's saying she's going to be famous. My best friend, a famous dancer—it's almost too incredible to believe.

Chloe's instant success does seem to come at a price, though. Many times during the course of the night I've noticed some of her fellow ballet students shooting dirty looks in Chloe's direction, especially when Dr. Friel fawns over her. It's sad that everyone's so insecure, so competitive that they can't be happy for one of their own.

Kirsten sleepily tucks a red velvet pillow under her head and starts to doze off. The next thing I know my eyes are drooping, too, and I'm sinking down on the couch. I let myself slip into the deliciousness of sleep only a few seconds at a time, fighting to stay conscious enough so that I can be fully alert in a matter of seconds.

A few minutes later, while I'm weaving between both states, I feel the heavy thud of bodies plopping down on the couch that's pushed up against the back of ours. The movement nudges me toward wakefulness. I look at Kirsten, but she's still sleeping soundly, completely undisturbed.

"I wish Madame would hurry up. I want to go home," I hear a girl say.

"She says we can leave when she's done—whatever that means," the other one says.

I recognize the whiny voices almost immediately. They belong to the girls who were wrestling at the bottom of the stairs when I first arrived. Throughout the evening I've bumped into the two girls dozens of times and was even in the cross fire when they started a short-lived food fight in the hallway with a dish of olives. I let myself drift back to sleep, imagining the mess we're in for if the waiters offer them some of the deviled quail eggs.

"Did you get to talk to him?" one of them say.

"No," the other one answers, "you-know-who was hogging him all night."

"What a brownnoser."

"You're telling me. She thinks she can make the corps just by kissing up to everybody."

"She *is* pretty talented, though," the first girl says. "It's not *all* talk."

The second girl snorts like a bull. "Believe me, she's no better than anyone else—she just knows how to fake it. If you've got enough attitude, you can make people think you're more talented than you really are."

I pull myself out of my sleepy state and turn an attentive ear to the catty twosome. For a second there, it almost sounds like they're talking about Chloe, but I quickly dismiss the idea. Chloe's no faker, and she's certainly not a brownnoser.

"Even if it *is* all attitude, it doesn't matter," the first girl says. "If the director and everyone else loves her, then she's going to get into the corps."

"Not *everyone* loves her," the second girl says, lowering her voice.

"What do you mean?"

I strain to listen.

"I have some pretty interesting info, if you can be trusted," she says in a confidential tone.

"Tell me! I want to know!"

The second girl pauses for a second or two, leaving both of us on edge. "I've heard that Madame has been pretty mad at Chloe these days . . . "

My eyes suddenly open wide with alarm.

"It seems as though everyone's favorite diva hasn't been paying the rent for the last few months, and Madame is getting fed up."

"You're kidding!"

"You know how Chloe is," the first girl says. "She spends all her money trying to look good and impress people, but I'm telling you, it's going to blow up right in her face."

A burning fear spreads through me. Is this girl really telling the truth, or is it some silly rumor that has taken on a life of its own?

"I'd like to see that," the other girl says.

"Shut up—here she comes . . . " A few seconds later, the girl's voice changes from a snarling, jealous growl to a sickly sweet tone. "Hi, Chloe! Having a good time?"

"Great time," Chloe answers. "Have you guys seen my friends?"

"No," the other girl says, "but I love that dress you're wearing. It's very chic."

"Oh, you like it? I bought it yesterday," Chloe answers, sounding flattered. The conversation makes me cringe. Chloe has no idea that these two were ripping into her just a few seconds ago.

"It must've been expensive," the chief gossiper

114

says, taking obvious delight in the hidden significance of her comment.

"Well, it wasn't cheap," Chloe says, laughing, "but you have to pay for quality."

Okay, I've had just about enough of this cruel little game of theirs. . . . I sit up and poke Kirsten's leg with my toe to wake her up.

"Oh, there you are!" Chloe says. "I was starting to think the two of you left without me!"

I'm sure you can imagine the jaw-dropping, eye-popping, complexion-paling expressions on the gossiping girls when they see me rise up from what they must've thought was an empty couch. The girl with the short, dark hair is trembling, which leads me to believe that she's probably the worst offender.

"Were you sleeping?" Chloe asks me.

A look of hope flashes across their faces.

"Not really," I say, glaring at the girls, "I was just resting my eyes. There were too many interesting conversations going on to fall asleep."

The dark-haired one suddenly gets this alarmed look on her face like she just accidentally swallowed glass. "It's getting late . . . we have to get going . . . " She grabs the other girl's arm, and they fly down the stairs toward the front door.

"Bye, guys," Chloe calls after them. She turns to me, her face glowing. "What about you and Kirsten. Are you guys ready to leave?"

"Yeah," I say, standing up, "let's get out of here."

As much as I don't want to believe the gossip, I find myself lying awake the rest of the night, wondering if it really is true. It seems impossible to me that Chloe would shove aside her love of dance to get caught up in all the shallowness and egotism, and yet, it would explain a lot of things. Like why Chloe felt the need to lie to Madame about shopping. If she wasn't paying her rent, then of course she didn't want to be seen spending any money. And then there was the Madame herself, telling me how distracted Chloe has been. Bit by bit, the pieces seem to fit, but the picture doesn't make any sense. No sense at all.

So while I'm lying there on the floor, thinking about things, I come to the conclusion that I'm going to have to do something about the situation on my own. That's when I come up with my plan.

Chloe gets up shortly after sunrise, a bright, cheery ball of energy, anxious to get the day started. "Time to get up, ladies," she says, throwing back the curtains. "We have a big day ahead of us."

I shield my eyes from the morning light. "What's going on?"

"I thought we'd take a tour of Alcatraz," Chloe says. "I've always wanted to go, and it's supposed to be fun."

"A tour of an old prison?" I say. "Sounds uplifting."

Kirsten rolls over, and the scarf filled with last night's shrimp suddenly makes an appearance from underneath her shoulders.

Chloe gasps. "Phew! What reeks in here?"

"It's Kirsten's shrimp purse."

"Shrimp purse? What's a shrimp purse?" she asks, throwing open the window.

I tuck the expensive and smelly scarf safely out of sight under Kirsten's pillow. "You really don't want to know," I tell her. "So you want to go to Alcatraz, huh? Shouldn't you be practicing your routine for the audition? It's only a couple of days away."

"I don't like to overpractice—it makes the routine stale," Chloe says. "As it is, I could already do it blindfolded. The best thing for me to do is just relax and enjoy myself."

This approach to an upcoming audition is definitely new for Chloe. Ever since I've known her, she has always spent the few days before an audition practicing to the point of exhaustion—hardly taking enough time to even eat or sleep.

"Get up," Chloe says. "Let's get going!"

I roll over onto my stomach and rest my head on my arms. "I don't think I'm going to go, Chloe, but I'm sure Kirsten will be up for it if you can ever drag her out of bed."

She stops making the bed and looks at me, her eyebrows knitting together. "Is there something wrong? We don't have to go there if you don't want to."

"It's not that. I'm just not feeling too good today. I didn't sleep well last night."

"We could stay here, instead," Chloe suggests. "We could have a picnic in the park and just hang out."

"If it's okay with you, I'd rather just spend the day by myself."

"Oh . . . all right." Chloe tries to look like she's okay with what I just said, but I know it must've really hurt her feelings. I wish I could explain my reasons to her, but I can't. I have to remind myself that it's best not to say anything now. It's for her own good.

As soon as Chloe and Kirsten leave for the day, I pull a pair of wrinkled khakis and a white shirt out of my pack and rummage through Chloe's closet until I find a small travel iron. Using Chloe's desk as a makeshift ironing board, I try to smooth out the wrinkles, but it doesn't seem to work too well because the iron never gets hot enough to even sting my finger when I touch it. After nearly a half hour of wasted effort, I put on the ensemble as it is, grab my leather travel journal so I look official, and hope for the best.

The thing about looking for a job is, well, I don't have a clue as to how I'm supposed to go about doing it. I had a job making pizza in high school at Poppa Roni's, but I think that all came about because my dad knew the owner, so you can't count that as any sort of real-world experience. Yesterday's paper was chock-full of serious kinds of jobs, like openings for accountants and secretaries, but no ordinary, short-term jobs. It seems like the only thing to do is to try my luck pounding the pavement. Whatever happens, I figure I can at least chalk it all up to a learning experience.

The first place I come across is a small juice bar on the corner, which looks hardly bigger than my bedroom at home. It doesn't seem like much of a place, but I figure if I want to help Chloe pay her rent and earn myself a little cash on the side, I'm in no position to be choosy.

Inside, folky music blares from the large speakers hanging precariously from wires attached to the walls. There are no people in the bar except for the two guys behind the counter who have the slouchy, carefree demeanor of college frat boys but who are old enough to start having grandkids.

The guy behind the counter with a bandanna tied around his head smiles lazily at me. "What can I do ya for?" he says. "Carrot-orange? Or are you more of a beet-parsley type?"

Even though it's around seventy-five degrees, my fingers are as cold as ice cubes. I can't believe how nervous I am. "Actually, neither," I say in a low voice virtually drowned out by the music.

"I knew you were way off," the other guy says as he peels huge carrots, the dusty outer surface cut off in long, thin strips. "Look at her, she's pale. She wants a flu-buster with a scoop of soy protein."

Being called pale doesn't exactly inspire confidence, and for a second I'm tempted to just buy a stupid juice and get the heck out of there. But I decide instead to think of this as a test run. I've got nothing to lose.

"I'm not here as a customer," I say, trying to control the quiver in my voice. "I'm looking for a job and wanted to know if you were hiring."

"Oh, no, sorry, honey," the bandanna guy says. "It's just the two of us here, and as you can see, business isn't exactly booming."

I nod, forcing the corners of my mouth into a smile. My insides are churning with rejection, even though this guy is as nice as can be. "Sure," I say. "I understand."

"Have you been looking at a lot of places?"

"This is the first one, actually," I say. "Do you know of any good places around here?"

The guy peeling carrots looks up at me. "There's a coffee shop around the corner you could try."

"Thanks," I say, heading for the door.

"Wait a second," the bandanna guy says. "Since you're already here, why don't we make you some juice on the house?"

"A little wheatgrass will put some rosy color on those pale cheeks of yours," the other guy says.

"All right," I answer, walking back to the counter. "Why not?"

Lessons numbers one and two from my job search experience come almost simultaneously. The first lesson is that wheatgrass tastes really bad; and the second lesson is that it leaves an ugly green stain if you spill it on your white shirt. I'd just left the juice bar with my complimentary juice, taken a sip of the nasty stuff (which tastes like liquid weeds, for those of you who are interested), and was making my way over to the nearest trashcan when some woman trying to catch a bus hit the cup with her elbow, popped the lid, and sent the foamy green juice dripping down the front of my shirt. Knowing it would take too long to go back to Chloe's place and find something else to wear, I trudge on to the coffee shop that the guy suggested, clutching my leather travel diary to my chest to cover the stain.

The coffee shop is actually more of an espresso bar and, unlike the lazy, third-world atmosphere of the juice place, it's hopping with people. There's a huge line of trendy twenty-somethings snaking alongside the pastry counter, then winding its way around the tiny, crowded café tables. The three people working behind the counter look wild-eyed, frazzled, and definitely in need of some help. Looks like I've come at the perfect time.

I get in line with everyone else and wait . . . and wait . . . and wait. By the time I finally get to the cashier, I've got my job search spiel down cold. I've been watching the workers and already I'm picking up a few things, like how to froth milk and where the different-sized take-out cups are kept. My heartbeat finally slows to a normal rate. I've got this one in the bag.

"Hi," I say to the cashier in my brightest, most confident tone, "my name is Miranda. I'm here to apply for a job."

I stick my hand out to shake the cashier's hand, but she just sighs, "I'll get the manager," and heads off toward a back room.

"Thank you," I answer. *So she didn't have the greatest personality, but that's okay,* I tell myself when I feel my confidence waning, *the only person who has to like you is the manager.*

The cashier emerges from the back room with a portly man in a short-sleeved dress shirt and a striped tie lumbering behind her. I take a deep breath and smile broadly, ready to wow him with my sparkling personality.

"I can see you're a busy man, so I won't take but a moment of your time," I say, looking him straight in the eye. "I noticed your establishment is a bit understaffed and I would like to offer my skills by becoming an employee."

Ha. I dare you to say no to that, Mr. Manager. . . .

"What kind of skills do you have?" he says, hitting me with a blast of onion breath. I try not to make a face.

"I'm great with people. You might even say that I'm a people person." I giggle, but the manager doesn't find it very funny. "I take direction well and I'm always on time. You can expect me to be prompt every single day. Oh, yeah—and dependable. I'm very dependable."

He looks at me with expressionless eyes and a mouth that prefers to stay in the neutral territory between a smile and a frown. "What about coffee?"

"No, thanks, I just had some wheatgrass juice a little while ago."

He looks annoyed. "I'm not asking if you *want* some coffee. I'm asking what do you *know* about coffee," he says, talking to me like I'm hard of hearing.

"Coffee . . . hmmm . . . " This was a question I hadn't banked on. "Well, there are many different kinds of coffee . . . regular, decaf, and many other kinds . . . some coffee is grown in Colombia . . . "

A few of the nearby patrons snicker. What I wouldn't give to be in Colombia myself right now.

"Thank you for that very informative answer,"

he says snidely, "but what I want to know is if you know how to make coffee. Can you operate an espresso machine?"

"Sure," I say, even though I've never touched one in my life, "I can do anything."

"Now we're getting somewhere," he says. "Let me take a look at your résumé."

An anxious tingle gnaws at the base of my spine. "Résumé?"

"You know, the piece of paper that lists your previous jobs."

"Well, that's easy, I worked at this pizza place—"

The tips of the manager's earlobes turn red. "I'd like to see it rather than hear it, if you don't mind."

I swallow hard. "The thing is, I'm staying with my friend and—"

"So you don't have one?" he interrupts.

"No . . . " I answer slowly.

The manager considers this for a second. "You came in here looking for a job without a résumé?" he says. "Why are you wasting my time?"

He turns on his heels and heads toward the back room. All of the customers and a few of the workers are staring. I'm so mad now, I'm beyond embarrassment.

"I feel bad for you," I call after him so everyone else can hear. "You just missed out on the best employee you'll never have!"

I have to take a break after the coffee bar incident because the tears start to flow and I can't get them to stop. Between my stained shirt and weepy, bloated face, I look like a wreck—not exactly the best way to make a good impression with prospective employers. Still, I decide to keep on trying. Like Chloe says, you've got to work it.

The next half dozen attempts aren't nearly as traumatic as my run-in with the manager, but they're just as disheartening. The clerk at the shoe store takes one look at me and nearly calls security, and everyone else I talk to simply says, "Thank you, we have all the help we need," while looking at me like I have three heads. I keep reminding myself that it's not a comment on my character, that they don't know anything about me, but it's hard not to take the rejection personally. It wears you out.

I'm thinking about going back to Chloe's and calling it a day when I spot a HELP WANTED sign in the window of a used bookstore. A bookstore—the thought of it alone makes me drool. It's a nice one, too, with a hand-built staircase of pine boards that leads to a loft of rare first editions. The door has a little brass bell attached to it that rings when customers walk in, and the whole place has a musty-dusty smell that reminds me of rainy days and my grandmother's closets. This place is perfect for me. I'd be crazy not to give it a try.

I ask the woman at the cash who I should speak to about the sign, and she points me to a middle-aged woman in the corner with silver-streaked hair and green eyeglass frames. "Hey, Margaret," the cashier calls to her, "this girl's here about the job."

Margaret straightens up from the box of books she's sorting through, a smile readily appearing on her face, but when she sees me, the pleasantness begins to fade. "May I help you?" she asks seriously, her eyes settling on the middle of my shirt.

I look down wearily, realizing that I'd dropped my arms and left the dark green stain in full view. I hug the travel journal to my chest to cover it up again. "Yes, I'm inquiring about the help wanted sign in the window."

"I see . . . " Margaret hesitates in the same way nearly every other person before her has, wondering what's the best possible way to say that they don't want to hire me. I can almost see the switch going off in her brain when the idea finally comes to her, but before she has the chance to say anything, I jump in.

"I know I look kind of frightening, but I've had a bad day. I really need a job and I think I would fit in perfectly here. I love bookstores and I love books, I'm easy to get along with and I'm a really hard worker."

Margaret's stare softens a little. "We need someone to shelve and catalog all our books. It's a rather dull job, I'm afraid."

"I don't care," I tell her. "I'll do anything."

"What is your name?"

"Miranda Burke."

Margaret nods. "Come with me, Miranda."

For once, maybe I'll catch a break. I follow Margaret to the back of the bookstore and into a small office. She sits behind an antique table covered with literary magazines and old newspapers. I pull up a straight chair and sit down.

"I'm not always such a sloppy dresser," I tell her, pointing to the stain. "Some woman hit me with her arm when she was trying to catch the bus."

"People are always in such a hurry these days," Margaret says, seeming relieved that there was an explanation. I can feel her slowly warming up to me. "So tell me, Miranda, are you in school?"

"I just graduated from high school."

Margaret smiles. "Congratulations. Will you be heading off to college in the fall?"

"I'm taking a little time off for myself right now."

"That's nice." Margaret doesn't seem turned off by my answer, which is a huge relief. "Have you worked in a bookstore before?"

"No," I say, feeling my tense muscles beginning to loosen, "but I've spent an awful lot of time in them. Bookstores are like a second home to me."

"I've always felt that way, too," Margaret says. "That's why I decided to open one of my own."

"I think about that sometimes—what it would be like to own a bookstore," I tell her. "Is it hard?"

Margaret shrugs and laughs. "I suppose having your own business always is—but I enjoy it." She pauses for a moment while I wait patiently for her next question. "You know, Miranda, I have a good feeling about you."

There's nothing Margaret could've said at this very moment that could've made me feel any better. "Thank you."

She moves aside some papers and finds a clipboard with a form on it. "Fill this out," she says, handing it to me. "I want to see just a few other applicants before I make my decision."

"Of course, I understand."

"But at the moment, I'd say things are looking in your favor," she says.

I smile. "At least *something*'s in my favor today."

Margaret laughs and stands up. "I'm going

back out to shelve some more books while you're filling out the application. If you have any questions, please feel free to ask."

"Okay, thank you."

When Margaret's gone, my eyes start to tear up with relief. *I got a job on my own,* I think proudly. *I really can take care of myself.*

Wiping away the tears, I get to work on the form. Name. *That's easy enough.* Date of birth. *Duh.* Social Security number. *They're getting harder, but I'm not stumped yet.* Phone number. *Well, I don't exactly have one of those. I'll just put a line through it.* Address ... address ... *okay, that one is a little bit tougher. I could put down Chloe's address, if I knew what it was, but Kirsten and I have to be moved out the day after tomorrow. I'll leave it blank.*

When I'm done with the rest of the form, I take it off the clipboard and proudly present it to Margaret at the front of the store. She nods and pouts her lower lip while she looks it over. "I notice you left the address line blank," she comments.

"Yeah, I didn't know what to put," I say. "I'm sort of between places right now."

"Moving out of your parents' house, huh?"

"No, actually, I'm staying with a friend," I tell her. "I've been doing a lot of traveling over the last few months. I just arrived in San Francisco a few days ago."

Margaret looks at me over the top of her glasses. "Where are you from, Miranda?"

"Connecticut."

"Do you plan on going back anytime soon?"

"Oh no, definitely not." I shake my head. "I took a year off from school to get away from Connecticut."

She nods. "So San Francisco is going to be your new home?"

"I don't know about that," I tell her. "I haven't really thought that far ahead."

Margaret pinches her lips together in thought. "It looks like we have a problem, then."

My forehead tightens. "What problem . . . ?"

"Well, I'm looking for someone who will stay here for a long time," she says. "I don't want to hire you and then wonder when you're going to leave."

Panic burns my throat. "I might stay. I don't know yet. I'd be a great employee for you no matter how long I stay."

"I'm sure you would be," she says, "but looking for someone is just too hard. I don't want to be interviewing people a month from now."

I clutch my journal so tightly against me that my knuckles are turning white. I'm so close right now, I can't give up without one more try. "Margaret, please, I really need a job."

"I'm sorry, Miranda," she says, folding my application in half. "It's not going to work out."

Back at Chloe's, I take a shower and lounge around in her room, feeling depressed. It was only one day of job hunting—not much time at all—and already I feel like a loser. Kirsten and Chloe weren't concerned at all about Madame's threat to kick us out, but what if she's not kidding? I mean, what's going to happen to us?

It's funny how when you're feeling bad about one thing, everything else starts looking grim, too. Like, just yesterday I was thrilled that I had made it here to California, but now it just feels way too far from home. It's been months now since I've been back, just long enough for my family to get used to life without me being around. I'm sure I must cross their minds much less than I used to— and I know that I'm too wrapped up in my own life to think about them all the time, either. Even though it used to bug me to death when my parents knew every little thing about me, I now can see the comfort in it. Now they know almost nothing about what's happened to me in the last few months, except for the little bits of information I feed them during our brief phone calls. There are so many pieces that end up getting left out. My biggest fear is that when I finally do go home again, both my family and I will have changed so much, we'll be like strangers to each other.

I drag myself off of Chloe's bed and start cleaning up the floor where Kirsten's and my stuff is strewn all over the place. The first thing to go is Kirsten's smelly shrimp-filled silk scarf that would bring Chloe to tears if she ever saw what Kirsten had done with it. Kirsten's never been the most thoughtful person. I suppose I should be happy that the two of them are at least getting along.

I glance at my cocktail dress, draped over the back of Chloe's desk chair last night when I came home too tired to hang it up. What an amazing party it had been—that is, until the very end, when those two girls were tearing Chloe apart behind her back. I pick the dress up, feeling the cool, expensive material slipping between my fingers, and know almost instantly that there couldn't possibly be any truth to the rumor that Chloe hasn't been paying her rent. Sure, Chloe likes to spend money, but she would never be so irresponsible as to throw money away if she couldn't cover a need as basic as rent. That's just not the kind of person she is.

As I put the dress back up on the hanger, I notice a piece of paper falling, fluttering down to the floor. TOP-NOTCH CATERERS, INC.—WHEN ELEGANCE IS THE ONLY OPTION . . . It's the business card Spencer gave me last night.

"I hope you're not sitting by the phone, Spencer, because this girl's taken," I say to myself, tossing the card in the wastebasket. The words send a delicious chill right down the middle of my back. I've never been in a position to say *that* before.

But just as I step away, a thought suddenly occurs to me. I return to the wastebasket and dig through the crumpled papers and old shrimp until I find the card. I smile to myself, shoving it in my pocket, and head downstairs.

Two steps from the door, I hear Madame's voice calling after me from somewhere in the parlor.

"Miranda," she calls to me, "I want to speak to you."

Gingerly touching the doorknob, I turn it slowly and ease the door open just wide enough so that I can slip through without being heard. But Madame is not fooled. "Don't pretend not to hear me. I know you do."

Groaning inwardly at my foiled escape, I close the door and follow the sound of Madame's creaky voice to the open door of the parlor, where she sits in a straight-backed chair facing the window. Her white skin glows like a ghostly apparition. I'm starting to wonder if she can actually see through walls. "How did you know it was me?" I ask, slightly creeped out.

"I heard the rhythm of your walk as you came down the stairs," she says. "Don't stand so far away. Have a seat near me."

Nervously, I toy with the corners of the business card. "I'd love to, but there's something urgent I need to take care of—"

"It wasn't a question," Madame says.

With a reluctant sigh, I do what she asks.

Madame doesn't look at me but keeps staring out the window. "I thought you would've been gone by now."

"You gave us three days—you said we wouldn't have to be out until Monday," I answer.

"I was being courteous," she says. "I expected you to give me the courtesy of leaving sooner."

I roll my eyes to the ceiling and let my shoulders droop, the same way my little sister Abigail does every time my mom asks her to clean her room. "I'm sorry, Madame, but I'm not up on my etiquette. I already explained to you that we have nowhere else to go."

Madame folds her hands demurely on the lap of her billowy skirt. "It's too bad that Chloe isn't going to make it into the company. She would've been a brilliant ballerina—one of the best."

I bolt out of my chair like a spring. Ever since my confrontation with the manager of the espresso bar and losing that bookstore job, my temper's been boiling, and I'm ready to blow up at the first person who asks for it.

"You have no right to say that about Chloe!" I explode. "Everyone else says she's going to make it except you. I think the only reason why you're so down on Chloe is because . . . well, because you're jealous!"

Madame stares at me with a stony face, but her eyes can't hide the pain I've caused. I feel instant regret for what I've said—not so much out of fear for what Madame could do to me or Chloe, but because my words were needlessly cruel. It doesn't matter if Madame is jealous or not—I should've kept my mouth shut.

"Are you done?" Madame asks evenly, her voice unchanging.

"Yes."

"Good," she says. "Sit."

I sit back down.

"Miranda, I am not trying to be unreasonable," she says. "Perhaps you think the things I say are unreasonable because you, like a lot of people, cannot see beyond what is directly in front of your face. Yes, I am no longer young, I can't help that. If I'm occasionally bitter it is because I am frustrated at the things I see that I cannot change. But I can assure you, I am not jealous of Chloe's talent."

I search Madame's face for understanding. "Then why are you so certain she's not going to make the corps? It's almost like you're *hoping* she'll fail."

Madame turns to me with sad, dark eyes. "I would never hope for such a thing."

She falls silent for a long time, and I grow more confused than ever. The anger in my heart turns to pity as I begin to wonder if Madame isn't acting out of maliciousness but because her mind is starting to go. My whole body feels heavy and sad, and a little bit frightened of her.

When it seems clear that she has nothing more to say to me, I stand up again. "I'm going to go now," I say, my voice much more gentle this time.

Madame draws in a raspy breath. "Remember, Miranda, to be a good friend, we mustn't always cup our hands and tread water nicely, but rather, spread our arms wide and make waves."

"Okay," I say, backing out the door, "I'll remember that."

Hello . . . may I please speak to Spencer?"

"Whom may I say is calling, please?" the voice says on the other end of the line.

"Miranda." I lean my heavy head against the side of the pay phone while I wait for the call to be transferred. It only takes about two seconds before I hear a husky voice.

"Hello, Miranda?"

"Spencer?"

"That's me," he says.

My stomach tingles. "I don't know if you remember me, but I was the one—"

"Wearing the green dress last night," he finishes. "Of course I remember you. I was hoping you'd call."

"Well, yes . . . " In my mind's eye I can picture him smiling at me with those gorgeous dimples. "But I'm not calling for the reason you might think. I know this is weird, because you hardly know me, but I need a favor."

"I told you I was a nice guy," he says. "What do you need?"

"I really need a job," I tell him. "Is there any way I could work for the catering company?"

"Oh, so you don't want to go out with me, huh?" he says in a teasing voice. "You just want to use me to get a job?"

A thin film of sweat breaks over my upper lip. "It's not that I don't want to go out with you. I mean, I *have* a boyfriend . . . but if I didn't, I'd definitely go out with you. . . ."

Spencer pauses for a beat or two. "You're not just saying that because you want a job, are you?"

"No—it's the truth," I gush. "You're gorgeous."

"I'm gorgeous, huh?" he says.

I blush deeply. Maybe that was the wrong thing to say. "So, do you think you can help me get some work?" I ask.

"Maybe. I know the owner pretty well," he says. "If you want, I could set up an interview."

I exhale happily. "That would be great, Spencer."

"You know, I've never liked my name, but it sounds good when *you* say it."

A burst of heat breaks over me. I gloss over his comment and move on to my next question. "When should I come by? Right now?"

"Actually, we're getting ready for a party," he says. "How about tomorrow afternoon? Just drop by whenever."

I write down the address he gives me. "What should I wear to the interview?"

"How about that green dress of yours?"

"It's a cocktail dress," I tell him. "I don't think that would make the right impression."

"It made quite an impression on *me*," he whispers into the phone.

"Okay, Spencer," I say tartly, trying to remove any hint of softness in my voice that could be misconstrued, "thanks so much for helping me out. I really appreciate it."

"Tell you what," he says, "if you get the job, you can take me out to thank me."

I let out a nervous laugh. "I don't think my boyfriend would like that very much."

"I'll promise not to tell if you won't."

"Okay, well it was nice talking to you." Before Spencer can say another word, I hang up on him.

"Oh brother," I wonder out loud. "What did I just get myself into?"

At the end of what seemed to be an endlessly long day, I finally met up again with Kirsten and Chloe back at the house. Chloe treats us to her favorite sushi restaurant in Japantown, where we are brought into a semiprivate room with rice paper walls. The three of us sit crosslegged on richly embroidered pillows at low tables while dainty waitresses in kimonos bring us lacquered trays arranged with pretty pieces of raw fish and vegetables covered with moist rice, then rolled in thin sheets of black-green seaweed called *nori*. The restaurant is very nice and relaxing, but my only complaint is that I wish Chloe would've warned me ahead of time that we would have to take our shoes off at the entrance. If I had known, I would've worn cleaner socks.

"The coolest part of the tour was when the guide made us crowd into the prison cells," Kirsten says. "After we were all in, they closed the doors on us—just for a minute or two. It was fun, but a few people started freaking out."

Chloe laughs. "There was this one guy in the cell across from us who grabbed the bars and started screaming 'I'm claustrophobic, let me out!' And then Kirsten yells back, 'If you're claustrophobic, then you shouldn't have gone in there in the first place!' Everybody was cracking up."

"Well, he wouldn't shut up," Kirsten adds. "Little kids were freaking out. I *had* to say something."

"Absolutely," Chloe says. "Someone had to set the guy straight."

I spread a little ball of a green horseradish paste called *wasabi* on my avocado roll. It's so pungent, it makes my nose feel like it's exploding. "I guess I missed a pretty fun day."

"You did," Chloe says pointedly. "So what did *you* end up doing?"

"I looked for a job," I answer casually.

Kirsten nearly spits out a mouthful of her miso soup. "That's why you didn't go with us? You were looking for work? Girl, you need your head checked."

Chloe couldn't have looked at me any weirder than if I had taken the votive candle from the table and tried to set my hair on fire. "What do you need a job for?"

"I'm running out of money," I tell her. "Plus, after Monday, Kirsten and I will need to find a place to stay."

Setting her chopsticks down across the tray,

Chloe dabs the corners of her mouth with a napkin and wrinkles her forehead at me. "You're still hung up on this Madame thing, aren't you?"

"She talked to me again today," I tell her. "I was on my way out the door when she caught me."

Chloe shakes her head. "Not again."

"What did she say?" Kirsten asks.

There's no way I'm getting into the entirety of the conversation—especially with Chloe's big audition only being a day or so away. Despite how cool she's been about the whole thing, Chloe has a very superstitious side when it comes to performing. Hearing that Madame doesn't think she'll make the corps would be a bad omen for Chloe, and I don't want to be responsible for her losing confidence.

"Madame told me she thought Kirsten and I would've moved out by now," I say, rearranging a pile of pink pickled ginger with my chopsticks. "She wants us gone by Monday."

"She's such a witch," Kirsten snarls.

"Ignore her," Chloe says to me. "Like I said, she's all talk."

"I don't think it was just talk," I answer. "She meant it."

Chloe turns to Kirsten. "Have you noticed how much Miranda likes to worry? I think it's a hobby of hers."

Kirsten nods knowingly. "Miranda's not happy unless she's miserable."

143

"Thanks for the psychoanalysis, guys," I say, disguising my irritation with a forced laugh. "Okay, forget about the whole Madame thing. I still need some money—which is why I'm going for an interview tomorrow at Top-Notch Caterers."

"Who are they?" Chloe asks.

"They catered the party last night."

A light clicks on behind Kirsten's slate-blue eyes. "You called Spencer, didn't you? This is starting to make a lot more sense. . . . "

Chloe grabs my arm. "Who's Spencer?"

"He's one of the waiters," I explain. "And no, Kirsten, it's not what you're thinking."

"It isn't?" she answers with mock innocence. "I knew you'd stray. I just didn't think it'd be so soon."

"What is she talking about?" Chloe asks.

I toss my napkin down on the table. "Ignore Kirsten—she's just trying to be funny."

Kirsten rolls a piece of tuna in a shallow dish of soy sauce and pops it in her mouth. "Spencer asked Miranda out on a date and gave her his card," she says. "You should've seen him—he was practically undressing her with his eyes."

"He was not!" I shout, loud enough to make the people at the next table look up to see what's going on. On one level, I'm offended by Kirsten's comment, but on another, I'm slightly intrigued, if not a little flattered. Did she really think he was looking at me that way? I'd love to ask her, but she'll just think I like him and then I'll never hear the end of it.

"You're not actually going out with this guy, are you?" Chloe asks.

"Of course not—it's a job interview."

"I wonder what kind of work he has in mind," Kirsten says with a sly grin. She pokes her fingers in her cheeks and makes dimples, imitating him. "Excuse me, Miranda, when you're done sweeping the floor I need you to come over here and make out with me."

"And while you're doing that, could you be so kind as to rip off my shirt and squeeze my biceps?" Chloe adds.

The two of them suddenly break into hysterics, laughing so hard that they slump against one another. Tears run down Kirsten's face, and Chloe starts wheezing, the air whistling out of her like a teakettle. Kirsten then smacks Chloe on the back to help her catch her breath, which only makes Chloe laugh even harder and brings on even more wheezing. It's a vicious cycle.

Soberly, I continue to rearrange the ginger slices, glad to have amused them both.

Despite Spencer's request, I show up for the interview not in my green dress but wearing my same old pair of khakis and a conservative black cashmere sweater set that Chloe let me borrow. I also pull back my hair in a severe bun and forgo any makeup I might've considered wearing, just so I look as serious and conscientious as possible. Wearing no makeup also has the added benefit of cooling down Spencer's interest in case we should run into one another.

Top-Notch is located on the eleventh floor of one of the high-rise buildings downtown. When the elevator doors open, I find myself in a sunny, cheery space with glass walls separating the professional kitchens from the reception area. Through the glass I see one chef rolling an enormous mass of dough into a thin sheet, while another decorates a wicker basket with roses and ivy.

"May I help you?" the receptionist asks.

"Yes," I answer with a smile. "I'm here for a job interview with the owner."

"Have a seat, please," he says, motioning toward a nearby couch. He dials a number on the phone, then announces my arrival. "Mr. Patrick will be out in just a minute."

"Thank you."

Back in the kitchen I notice the chef is sprinkling the dough with fresh herbs and cheese, then cuts the dough into long, thin strips and rolls them up like cigars. My guess is that she's making cheese straws, like the ones they served last night at the party. A warm, contented feeling settles in my stomach. While books are my first love, food and cooking has always run a close second. Maybe the bookstore job didn't work out for a reason. Maybe this could turn into something really big for me.

"Miranda—it's so nice to see you."

I look up to see Spencer standing over me, wearing blue jeans and a preppy, button-down shirt. He looks so different from how he did the other night now that his blond hair is lit by the sun and he's not wearing a tux. I wish I could say he doesn't look nearly as good, but the truth is, I think he's even more handsome than I remember.

I smile at Spencer with my lips closed, thinking that if I don't show any teeth, maybe he won't think of it as a come-on. "Hi, Spencer. I didn't recognize you without a tray in your hand."

I must've hit his funny bone square-on because he's suddenly doubled over, laughing. When

Spencer finally gains his composure, he stands there staring with the same puppy-dog look Dustin used to get just before he kissed me.

"Shall we go in the back office and talk?" he says, clearing his throat.

"No, I don't think that would be such a good idea," I say, primly clutching my travel journal. "I'm waiting for Mr. Patrick."

A mysterious smile curves Spencer's full lips. "*I'm* Mr. Patrick."

At first I think he's joking, but the receptionist confirms it with a nod.

"Oh, okay," I say. "Is the owner coming by soon to interview me?"

The receptionist raises his eyebrows and nods in Spencer's direction again.

My jaw drops to the floor. "You mean *you're* the owner?"

"Let's go to the office and talk," Spencer says, helping me to my feet. I follow him around a corner to a big carpeted office with massive windows that have a perfect view of the downtown area. It's a far cry from Margaret's little back room in the bookstore.

"Have a seat, Miranda," Spencer says, sitting behind a mahogany desk with brass fixtures.

"I don't get it," I say, falling into an elegantly carved chair that looks like it belongs in a museum. "You were carrying around trays last night. You were waiting on people."

"One of my waiters didn't show up, so I filled in," Spencer says. "Sometimes I just do it because I like to move through the party and see if the guests are enjoying themselves."

On the shelf behind Spencer's desk I spot a framed photo of him shaking hands with a famous chef I recognize from a cooking show on TV. "I hope you don't mind me saying this, but you look a little young to be the owner of such a successful business."

"I'm twenty-seven. I started the business five years ago after I graduated from cooking school," Spencer says. "My parents are big on the social circuit. They know practically everyone in town—which got the business off the ground in a hurry."

I'm still sitting there, blinking with disbelief, when Spencer suggests we get the interview rolling. "So, Miranda, have you ever worked in catering before?"

"Never, Mr. Patrick."

"How about waiting tables? Have you ever done that?"

"Not that I recall."

Spencer leans back in his chair and plays with a silver pen that I'm sure cost more than my train ride from Colorado. "Have you ever worked in the food service industry in any capacity whatsoever?"

"No—wait, yes I have," I say. "I used to make pizza at a place called Poppa Roni's."

"Poppa Roni's, huh?" Spencer narrows his

green eyes. "Fascinating. Tell me more about this *Poppa Roni's* . . . "

"Well, the dough was already made—it came in trucks every week, frozen, and we'd have to thaw it out in the fridge overnight," I tell him. "When a customer ordered a pizza, we'd grease the pans with this solid shortening–type stuff that came in cans, then we'd press out the dough, cover it with canned sauce, then shredded cheese, and whatever toppings they wanted."

Spencer nods slowly. "And what sort of toppings would there be?"

"Sausage, peppers, mushrooms . . . "

"Did you become familiar with anchovies?" Spencer's expression is deadpan, but I know he's not taking any of this seriously.

"Quite familiar," I say, struggling to keep a straight face. "You might say I have a great deal of anchovy experience."

"Let's see . . . you have no catering experience and no waiting experience, but you have a great deal of anchovy experience . . . " Touching his finger to his lips, Spencer falls silent for a moment. "You're hired."

"That's it?" I ask. "Don't you need to see a résumé or have me fill out an application or something?"

"That won't be necessary," he says.

"Are you sure?"

"Are you trying to talk me out of hiring you?"

"No," I answer, my heart leaping for joy. I'm so happy I want to jump up on his desk and plant a big wet kiss on one of those gorgeous dimples of his, but of course I refrain in the spirit of professionalism. "So, when can I start?"

"We have a party tomorrow night," he says. "Be here by four. Do you have a tux you can wear?"

"No," I answer.

Spencer tosses the pen onto his desk. "Oh, it doesn't matter. We'll get one for you."

I can't help it, I'm beaming. "Thank you so much, Mr. Patrick. You have no idea how much you're helping me."

Leaning forward on his elbows, Spencer smiles at me from across his desk. "Now that I got you a job, I guess that means you can take me out and thank me."

I shift a little in my seat, suddenly feeling put on the spot. "Like I mentioned before, I don't think my boyfriend would like that very much."

"Yeah, somehow I remember you saying that," he answers. "You don't have to do it if you don't want to. I just thought it would be fun."

"I'm sure it would be, but I just don't think it's a good idea," I say.

"You don't have to explain yourself," Spencer says, "I understand."

The sunlight coming through the windows suddenly feels very hot against the back of my neck. I stand up. "So I guess I'll see you Monday."

Spencer reaches out and takes my hand, but instead of shaking it he sort of holds it for a minute or two, his thumb softly rubbing the back of my knuckles. "I'll be looking forward to it," he says.

Chloe told me to meet her in one of the private rehearsal rooms at the school after my interview, where she's practicing her routine for tomorrow's audition to get into the ballet company. I get there in time to catch Chloe leaping through the air like a gazelle, her feet landing on the hardwood floor with the lightest touch, in perfect time to the piano music being played on a small tape player in the corner. As soon as she sees me in the mirror, she smiles, then clicks off the music.

"You don't have to stop," I tell her. "Keep practicing."

Chloe grabs a towel and wipes the dampness from her neck. "I was just about to take a break, anyway," she says. "How did the interview go?"

"I got the job," I say with an excited grin. "I start tomorrow night."

"That's fantastic!" she says, ever the supportive friend.

"It turns out Spencer is actually the owner—and he's only twenty-seven."

Chloe arches her eyebrows, obviously impressed. "And this guy has the hots for you? I bet he's got some serious bucks—you should go for it."

I give her an annoyed look. "Dustin's my guy, remember? What is it with you and Kirsten? You both know I already have a boyfriend, but you're after me to go for someone else."

"Don't get freaked, Miranda, we're just kidding around." Chloe pulls a sweatshirt over her leotard and sits on the floor.

"So how is practice going?" I ask, changing the subject.

"It's nothing—this stuff is so ridiculously easy," Chloe says. "It's kind of a joke, actually. I don't know why they're even making me audition."

I drop down on the floor beside her. "What do you mean?"

"I'm going to make it into the corps, anyway. It's a given." Chloe says this not out of bravado or arrogance, but like it's a pure, indisputable fact. "Dr. Friel says my chances look really, really good."

"Wait a second—I thought you had to perform in front of a bunch of people."

Chloe takes a swig from her water and offers it to me. "Right. There's a board of judges made up of instructors from the school and the company who decide who gets in and who doesn't."

"Okay, so if there's a bunch of people voting,

how can Dr. Friel know how they're going to vote ahead of time?" I ask.

Chloe sighs, seemingly agitated that I'm not taking Dr. Friel's comment at face value. "First of all, I've met just about every judge on the panel. Madame is one of them, and so are a bunch of Dr. Friel's colleagues who I met at the party the other night. That's why I did the rounds, so everyone would get to know me. Dr. Friel said they were very impressed."

"Excuse me for being dumb," I say, "but I don't see how meeting people at a party makes a difference at your audition."

"Stop being so literal, Miranda. It's not just about how well you perform—dance is such a small part of it," Chloe explains. "When I was in high school, it was just about the audition, but out here, there's a whole social structure you have to think about. Almost everyone in my class is a great dancer, but very few of them know how to put themselves out there, make contacts, and get known. Jeez, a lot of them don't even know how to carry on a decent conversation! The company isn't looking for a dancer, they want a *star*."

"Is that what you want? To become a star?" I ask.

"Heck, yeah," Chloe says, "and right now I'm the closest thing to it this school's got."

I sit in silent amazement, thinking about how easy everything has been for Chloe until this point. Ever since her first ballet class at the age of three, she's always known what she's wanted, always known what her talent was. And when she decided to study dance seriously, it seemed as though all the forces in the universe conspired to grant her everything she needed to accomplish her goals with as little effort as possible. Nothing has ever stood in her way.

"So what happens next?" I ask. "Once you get in the company, what do you do then?"

A dreamy and distant look comes over Chloe's heart-shaped face. "Well, first of all, I'll get to move out of the house and into an apartment, which is really cool. Then I'll get to go to all sorts of extravagant parties and fund-raisers—I can't wait for that. And pretty soon I'll need to start concentrating on pubic relations—you know, doing television interviews, charity work—all that good stuff."

"I meant as far as your dancing goes," I tell her. "What then?"

"Oh." Chloe laughs. "Well, they'll put me in the corps first—I'll be one of the background dancers. I should be able to work my way up to one of the principle dancers within a year or so."

"That's pretty ambitious of you," I say.

"You have to be ambitious in this business," Chloe answers, taking off her ballet slippers. "Oh, before I forget—your mom called my cell phone while you were out."

My eyes widen with alarm. "Is something wrong?"

"No, no," Chloe assures me, "she said she had some mail she wanted to forward to you."

"Mail? From whom?"

"I don't know." Chloe shrugs. "All she said was a package arrived yesterday and the postmark was from England."

My heart surges. "Oh, my God, Chloe," I say, squeezing her arm tight, "it must be from Dustin."

When Chloe comes back from the audition early the next day, her grin is as wide as the Pacific. "I *killed* in there," she says, recounting her routine move by move. "You should've seen the judges' eyes when I was done. I totally bowled them over—everybody except Madame, of course. She crossed her arms and scowled at me. She just loves to be difficult."

Kirsten and I throw our arms around Chloe and give her a huge hug. "You made it into the company—congratulations!" I say.

"Well, it's not *official* yet," Chloe says. "They're posting names this afternoon."

"Who wants to wait that long when we already know the outcome?" Kirsten says. "Let's go celebrate now!"

Our impromptu celebration takes on the form of a picnic on the green lawn surrounding the Palace of Fine Arts, a gorgeous copy of classical architecture that is made of papier-mâché and plaster instead of stone. You'd never know by looking at it, though, and the enchanting setting inspires the three of us to lounge on the grass and eat grapes, imagining ourselves as Greek goddesses who can control the destiny of man with the simple flick of our wrists. Kirsten casts a spell on all men with well-developed abs and a healthy wallet to fall in love with her at first sight. Chloe throws a curse on all her dance rivals, both present and future, while I'm a simple goddess commanding only that the winds bring Dustin back to me.

The three of us head back to the house in high spirits, linked arm in arm like sisters, happily awaiting the official launch of Chloe's career. But when we reach the front steps, we notice something strange. Both Kirsten and Chloe are shocked by it, but sadly I'm really not that surprised at all.

"What's my stuff doing outside?" Kirsten complains loudly, her backpack laid across the top step, the unzipped pockets overflowing with clothes. "I can't believe someone would dump our stuff outside."

"Mine's underneath it," I notice.

"I can't believe this," Kirsten rants. "I mean, anyone could've come along and stolen our stuff. If anything's missing, I'm getting a lawyer."

I give my pack a quick check. Nothing's been disturbed. "I hate to say this, guys, but I told you Madame wanted us out."

Chloe stamps her feet angrily. "This is ridiculous," she says, searching her purse for her keys.

"There's no way that old woman is going to treat *my* guests that way."

I stand there calmly while Kirsten goes through every pocket like there's a time bomb in it about to explode. So it's official now: Kirsten and I are out on our own. As annoying as the situation is, at least I can take comfort in the fact that I prepared for it by getting a job. And then there's also satisfaction in knowing that I'm not the neurotic worrywart Chloe and Kirsten made me out to be. From now on, maybe they'll start listening to me more.

"The stupid thing won't turn!" Chloe growls, jiggling her key in the lock. When the key refuses to budge, she smacks the door loudly with her hand. "The lock's broken—well, that's just perfect."

"Where's my silk scarf?" Kirsten says, rummaging through the pockets again. "I can't find my scarf."

The door suddenly opens, and the two bratty girls who had been gossiping about Chloe at the party come out. They seem absorbed in a contest of who can pull the other one's hair the hardest, but the second they see the three of us, they drop their fistfuls of hair and smile broadly.

"Thank goodness you guys are here," Chloe says, calming down a little. "The stupid lock is broken, and I couldn't get the door open."

"That's funny—my key works fine," one girl says, nudging her friend in the ribs.

"Mine, too," the other one says with a smug laugh. "Madame changed the lock because she said she wanted to separate the serious ballerinas from the amateurs."

Chloe's mouth tightens, and her eyes narrow. "What's that supposed to mean?"

An awful realization rattles deep within my bones, but I just stand there, not saying anything.

"I don't know," the second one says, shrugging. "You'll have to ask Madame yourself." The two continue to skip down the stairs happily while Chloe grabs the door before it shuts.

When the first girl reaches the bottom of the stairs, she stops and turns around. "Oh, by the way—sorry to hear about the audition, Chloe."

"Yeah," the other one chimes in, "you must be pretty upset."

Kirsten and I freeze. I swear I can almost see a sudden chill seize Chloe as she struggles to keep her composure. "Upset about what? It went great."

"Gee, that's funny," the first girl says, "because I didn't see your name on the list."

I look back at Chloe, expecting her to say something, but she's already gone, the door slamming shut behind her.

A minute later, Chloe opens the door again, in tears. "It's not there," she says, wiping her damp face with the back of her hand. "My name is not on the list."

"Maybe it was an oversight," I say, giving her a hug. "Like you said, everyone already knew you were going to get it—so maybe they forgot to put your name down."

"I don't think that's what happened," she cries.

Kirsten drops her bag on the step. "Is there someone you can talk to about it?"

Chloe considers this for a minute, then suddenly her red-rimmed eyes narrow and her jaw clenches tight. In an instant her energy seems to have taken a quick detour from sadness to mounting anger.

I swallow hard, a little frightened of this sudden transformation. "What is it, Chloe?"

"I was just thinking about Madame," she says, her voice turning icy, "the way she just sat there after my routine was over, with this hard look on her face. I bet it was her. I bet she's the one who didn't vote for me."

"I wouldn't be surprised," Kirsten says ruefully. "Sounds like something the old bat would do."

While Kirsten and Chloe were just speculating, I knew it was true. I remember my last encounter with Madame in the parlor, when she had seemed so certain that Chloe's future was doomed. *"It's too bad that Chloe isn't going to make it into the company,* she'd said. *She would've been a brilliant ballerina—one of the best."*

I had taken her words as idle, jealous talk, but little did I realize at the time that Madame was literally telling me what was going to happen. At the time, I didn't want Chloe to know what Madame had said out of fear it would break her concentration, but perhaps in keeping it a secret I had prevented Chloe from finding a way to defend herself against Madame's dirty tactics. My stomach tightens into a painful bundle of guilt. If I did something to harm Chloe's career, I don't think I can ever forgive myself.

Chloe grits her teeth, her hands clenched into tight fists. "I'm going to talk to that witch and find out what the story is."

"Are you sure that's a good idea?" I say, tugging at her wrist to hold her back. I can feel a trembling vibration travel down the length of her arm, like a volcanic fury rumbling inside her that's on the brink of explosion. "Let's think about this a little bit before you go in there. Maybe you should plan what you want to say first—"

"She already knows what she wants to say," Kirsten interrupts. "Just give that shriveled prune a piece of your mind."

I'd love to give *Kirsten* a piece of my mind right now, along with a good swift kick in the butt for adding more fuel to Chloe's raging anger. Kirsten's comment is all the encouragement Chloe seems to need, because she suddenly breaks away from me and goes back inside. This time, Kirsten and I follow behind.

A dissonant chorus of voices rises up from the parlor, where all the dancers have gathered to look at the list. Some of the girls are high-fiving each other and hugging while a few others skulk off with dejected looks on their faces. A few of the girls call out Chloe's name as she marches by the furor, but she won't so much as look their way. Instead, she heads straight for Madame's apartment, with a single purpose in mind.

"Chloe, slow down," I call, chasing after her. I wish she'd take a breather, just to cool down a little bit. A few careless words and who knows, she could damage her career forever.

Chloe ignores me and barges into Madame's apartment without knocking. Kirsten and I slip in behind her just in time to see Madame spooning some honey into her afternoon tea. The old woman is hardly startled by the interruption; in fact, judging from the empty teacup set out on the table, I'd say she's been expecting it.

"Have a seat, Chloe," Madame says, calmly pouring her a cup of tea. "Honey or lemon?"

"I don't want any of your stupid tea," Chloe barks, refusing to take a seat. "What I want is an answer from you."

Madame brings the cup up to her wrinkly lips and takes a sip. The room is so quiet, it's almost as if the three of us have stopped breathing.

"I don't talk to people who show a lack of respect," Madame says. "Now have a seat."

Chloe holds her ground for a few seconds before lowering herself into the chair. "Why isn't my name on the list?"

Madame offers a plate of tea cookies to Kirsten and me, still standing in the doorway. I politely refuse, and Kirsten doesn't say a word. She just glares at Madame with a stare that could give a polar bear the chills. Unfazed, Madame takes a cookie for herself. "You weren't ready," she finally says.

"That's a load of crap!" Chloe shouts, pounding the table with her fist. "I was more than ready—I could've done that dumb routine in my sleep!"

"It's true, your technique is exquisite," Madame says, "but I find you lacking in other essential areas."

Chloe looks up at me and shakes her head with

utter disbelief. "Okay, so where am I *lacking?*"

Madame takes a bite of cookie. "Well, you've shown a great disregard for my authority as well as for house rules. I also find that you lack a sense of responsibility toward yourself and others."

"I don't know what you're talking about," Chloe says.

"Chloe," Madame says, "don't pretend this is all new to you. We've had many discussions. I've given you plenty of warnings."

Up until this moment I'd thought it was best to keep my mouth shut, but now I feel a sudden need to interrupt. "Please don't blame Chloe for Kirsten and me staying here," I speak up. "We knew you wanted us to go—we shouldn't have stuck around. We'll be on our way, and everything can get back to normal."

Kirsten growls under her breath. I'm sure she has a few choice words of her own that she'd like to share with Madame, but thankfully she keeps them to herself.

"That's not the entire reason, though it is certainly a portion of it," Madame says. "If you'd care for a detailed list, Chloe, I'll speak to you in private. I wouldn't feel comfortable openly discussing anything that might embarrass you in front of your friends."

"I'm done talking to you." Chloe stands up, her normally delicate features twisted in a snarl. "I'm going to talk to Dr. Friel about the way you've been harassing me. He's not going to be happy about this *at all.*"

"You can talk to whomever you wish," Madame answers. She sets down her cup of tea and stares directly into Chloe's eyes, readily accepting the challenge. "Before you go, though, I recommend you pack an overnight bag. You may come back in a few days when you're more civilized to retrieve the rest of your possessions."

"You're the one who'd better start packing," Chloe threatens before storming out the door.

Kirsten follows quickly behind. I'm just about out the door myself when Madame stops me. "Miranda," she says, with trembling lips, "remember what we talked about. I hope you'll help Chloe now, when she needs you most."

I just look at her for a long moment, then head out the door.

"I apologize for dropping in so unexpect-edly," Chloe says politely.

Dr. Friel leads the three of us to a small grouping of furniture in a corner of his parlor, which seems all the more vast without a party going on. "Yes, well, it seems to be a day full of surprises, doesn't it?" he says in a cordial tone.

"I guess you already know why we're here," Chloe says somberly.

"I assume it's because of your audition," he says.

"It's more than that, actually." Chloe looks down at her hands, folded demurely in her lap. "I'd like to file a formal complaint against Madame Krakinov."

I expect Dr. Friel to be stunned by Chloe's announcement, but if he is, he shows no signs of it. Instead, he continues to smile gently at the three of us. "That's a rather weighty proposal, Chloe. Are you sure that's something you really want to do?"

Chloe's chin starts quivering. "Madame has had it in for me since the day I started."

"That can't be right," Dr. Friel says, crossing his legs. "I assure you that Madame is your greatest supporter."

"Chloe's telling the truth," Kirsten chimes in. "We've seen her pick on Chloe."

I just sit there, not daring to say anything.

"Outwardly, Madame might seem that way," Chloe says. She speaks slowly, as if she's taking great pains to choose the right words. "But when we're alone, she acts . . . differently."

Lines appear on Dr. Friel's forehead. "You're not suggesting that Madame is putting on a false front, are you?"

"I would never say that," Chloe says, suddenly backing down. "However, she is getting on in years. She's probably not even aware that she's doing it."

The cordial smile fades from Dr. Friel's lips. I notice a distinct chill in the room. "I've worked with Madame for many years, Chloe, and have a great deal of respect for her. You, on the other hand, have known her a matter of weeks. Forgive me if I trust my opinion of her over yours."

A startled look comes into Chloe's doelike eyes. She seems totally caught off guard by the fact that Dr. Friel isn't taking her side. We all are.

"Don't you think it's strange that she's the only one who didn't vote for me?" I can hear the panic rising in Chloe's voice. "Doesn't that seem unfair?"

"First of all, Madame wasn't the only one who voted against you," Dr. Friel answers.

Chloe's face looks so stricken by this piece of news that I instinctively reach out and give her hand a reassuring squeeze. "Who else?" she chokes.

"It would not be proper for me to name names," he says, "but I can tell you that I was one of them."

A sharp, audible intake of breath comes from Kirsten's side of the couch. No matter how hard Chloe had been struggling not to cry before, this sends her right over the edge. "But I don't understand," she cries in between taking shaky sips of air. "At the party, you said I was going to be a star. And before that, you told me my chances for getting in looked really good."

Dr. Friel sighs and rubs his forehead. "Looking back now, I think there was a definite lack of judgment on my part to build up your expectations. I apologize for doing that to you, Chloe. But I meant every word I said. You are extremely talented and bright—I had every reason to believe you'd make the cut. What I didn't know at the time was that there were some other issues of concern."

Chloe's poise dissolves into a puddle at Dr. Friel's feet.

"Like the rent, for instance," he continues.

"Madame told me that you're behind on the rent because you've been spending your money on expensive clothes and makeup. She has reason to believe, as well, that you are running up an enormous credit card debt."

So the rumor is true, I think grimly. *What are you doing to yourself, Chloe?*

Chloe dabs her eyes with the sleeve of her blouse. "I don't see how that's any of her business."

Dr. Friel ignores the comment and continues on. "You refuse to rehearse regularly with the others. You habitually show up to class late because you've stayed out the night before. You blatantly ignore house rules . . . shall I go on?"

Chloe doesn't answer.

"Sometimes we tolerate this sort of behavior at the school because the students are young and inexperienced," he says, "but the company is a different story. These are professionals—we can't be wasting their time with irresponsible corps members."

"I would be more responsible in the company," Chloe says, sniffling. "I've been acting that way because I'm so bored at the school."

Dr. Friel shakes his head. "No excuses, Chloe. The decision was based on the behavior you've demonstrated. I'm afraid you're going to have to live with it."

"All right, then," Chloe says, getting up to leave. "Thank you for your time."

I hate leaving Chloe after such a disastrous afternoon, but by the time we leave Dr. Friel's place, I already have to leave for my first day of work at the catering place. When I say good-bye to Chloe at the bottom of the hill, she looks pale and shell-shocked, like someone whose entire world just blew up in front of her. And I guess, in a way, it did.

When I arrive at Top-Notch, the elevator doors open to complete chaos—a scene very different from the tranquillity I witnessed yesterday when I came for my interview. Food carts whip past me from both directions with such speed and frequency that just stepping out of the elevator seems a lot like crossing the freeway at rush hour. The tuxedoed waiters scurry around in rambling, circular patterns carrying trays of delicate stemware and bags of ice. Add to that the frenzy of everyone shouting at once, and you get a good idea of what a madhouse it is.

In the middle of playing a game of chicken

with a watermelon boat (I'm the one who backs down, in case you're wondering), I spot Spencer directing various people where to go. Even with all the craziness around him, he notices me and instantly smiles, motioning for me to come over to him. "Hi, Miranda," he says, looking incredibly handsome in his tux. "You're a little late—was the traffic bad?"

I glance at the wall clock, confused. "I'm not late," I tell him. "You told me to come at four o'clock."

Spencer smacks his forehead. "My mistake. I guess I was just anxious to see you, that's all." A waiter carrying a box of cocktail napkins comes barreling through, and Spencer pulls me out of the way just in time before I get run over.

"You have to be careful," he says. "Just before an event, things can get a little crazy."

"What should I do?" I ask him, dodging a woman with a glass vase filled with roses.

"There's a rack of tuxes by the windows. Find the one with your name on it and change in the ladies' room around the corner," he says. "Also, you should pin back that beautiful red hair of yours—we don't want it falling into the food."

When I emerge from the ladies' room in my oversized tuxedo, feeling like a little kid who's just raided her dad's closet, I notice that Spencer's gone and everyone is heading for the elevators. Not knowing what to do next, I follow the crowd, wedging myself into one of the elevator cars between a carving station and a sheet cake that says HAPPY 60TH, HARRY in blue icing.

The event, as it turns out, is an office party for an accounting firm on the ninth floor of the same building. It's the owner's birthday, and his employees are throwing him a swank party on the company's tab. During the setup, with Spencer nowhere to be found, I try to ask a few people how I can help out but everyone's too busy to take the time to show me. And it's not the sort of thing that you can just step into—you really have to know what you're doing. So I stand in the corner, out of the way, waiting for someone to tell me what to do.

Just before the party's about to start, Spencer finds me and leads me into the office kitchen where the finishing touches are being put on the hors d'oeuvres.

"How are you doing so far?" he asks, pressing up against me to let a waiter by.

"I haven't really done much but stand around," I confess, my heart racing. I lift up a floppy tuxedo sleeve. "The monkey suit's a little too big."

"Here, take off the jacket," Spencer says, slipping it off my shoulders. "You can roll up the sleeves if you want. Is that better?"

I nod. "So what am I supposed to be doing?"

"You'll be passing out appetizers, just like I was doing at the party the other night. You hold the tray with one hand and a stack of cocktail napkins in the other like this." He demonstrates with a nearby platter of chicken skewers. "Is your balance good?"

"It's all right, I guess."

Spencer hands the platter to me. "You try it."

Bending my arm at the elbow, I balance the tray on the pads of my fingers, just like he did. Spencer moves up behind me to adjust my arm and show me the proper way to pass off a cocktail napkin with one hand.

"This looks pretty good," he says. His breath tickles the back of my neck. "Work your way through the crowd until the tray is empty, then come back for another one. Make sure you always know what you're serving in case someone asks. Got it?"

"Oh, yeah," I exhale, trying to ignore the tingle in my stomach. I can't decide whether the job is making me nervous or if it's the way Spencer keeps brushing up against me. "I've got it."

"Mr. Patrick," a waiter calls from the hallway, "we have a problem with the ice sculpture."

"I'll be there in a second," he calls back. "Okay, Miranda, I've got to go. Just be polite and smile at people and you'll do fine. If you need anything— a shoulder rub, a compliment, someone to gaze at you admiringly—just let me know."

"I'll keep that in mind," I answer, heading out into the party.

By the end of the night, my feet and arms are aching, and I can no longer tell the difference between a shrimp wonton and a beef kebab. There's a gangly accountant who's slumped in the corner, sleeping off whatever it was that gave him the courage to do the Macarena in front of all his coworkers while standing on the cheese table. I place a cocktail napkin by his head and leave my last appetizer for his breakfast.

Done . . . finally . . . I loosen my bow tie and drop off the silver tray in the kitchen, then slump into the nearest chair. I'm so exhausted, I never want to move again.

Spencer comes up and playfully hits me with a bar towel. "How are you doing?"

"My feet feel like they're about ready to burst out of my shoes," I complain. "But other than that, I'm all right. I had no idea this was such hard work."

"It's tough being on your feet for a long time," Spencer says, pulling up a chair opposite mine. He picks up my right foot and props it up on his knee, easing off my shoe. Then, holding my foot with both hands, he starts massaging my sole with his thumbs.

"Don't do that!" I squeal, jerking my foot away.

"Ticklish, are we?" he teases.

"A little," I say, jamming my foot back into my shoe. "I've got to get going, anyway."

Spencer rolls up the sleeves of his tuxedo shirt. "Where do you live?"

"I'm staying with a friend in the Haight."

"Is she picking you up?"

"No," I answer. "I thought I'd either walk or catch a bus or something."

"Not at this time of night, you're not," he says firmly. "I'll give you a ride."

"You don't have to," I protest. "I'll be fine, really."

Spencer pulls a key ring out of his pocket and twirls it around his finger. "Go get changed and then I'll take you back."

I'm far too drained to continue protesting, so I grab my stuff and change in the ladies' room. When I come back out again, Spencer says good night to the cleanup crew, and we head down to the lobby.

"We had a pretty good night," Spencer says, holding the door open for me as we step outside. "Those stuffed shirts racked up a nice little bar tab."

"They're definitely going to be paying for it tomorrow," I say, yawning. "I saw one guy passed out with his head in a trash can. I'd hate to be him tomorrow morning when he wakes up."

At some point during the party it must've rained, because the streets are slick and shiny, the streetlights reflecting on the damp pavement. Spencer walks up to a silver Porsche, disengages the car alarm, then unlocks the door for me.

"This is yours?" I ask, running my hand over the black leather upholstery.

Spencer starts the car and revs the engine. "Well, if it isn't, I have no idea how these keys got in my pocket," he teases. "You'd better buckle up."

"Right." I scarcely have enough time to do it before Spencer hits the gas. The car responds without even a second's hesitation, and soon we are zooming down the empty streets of San Francisco, hitting an endless string of traffic lights just as they turn green.

"So where do you live?" I ask, blinking back sleep as the city blocks whiz by us.

"I have a place on Russian Hill," Spencer says, shifting into third. "We could swing by there right now if you want."

"Uh, no," I say suddenly. "That's okay."

The hazy glow of passing streetlamps illuminate the contours of Spencer's face. "Don't sound so nervous—I don't bite."

"I know you don't," I giggle, even though I'm not really sure whether he does or not. "It's really late, and my friends are expecting me."

"Some other time, then," he says.

As we get closer to Chloe's place, I spot Kirsten's dumpy blue Escort with Jersey license plates parked on the street. "You can pull over right here," I tell him before we get too close.

The car stops on a dime. "Which one's yours?" Spencer says, scanning the row of apartment houses.

I point to the ballet residence. "That one over there."

"Nice," he says. "I bet it looks pretty nice inside, too."

"It is," I answer, giving him a sly glance.

Spencer unbuckles his seat belt. "Let me walk you to the door."

"I can walk just fine on my own, thank you," I whisper. My head feels thick and foggy, as if I'm in a daze.

He reaches into his pocket and pulls out an envelope. "Oh, before I forget—your pay."

The welcoming sight of $150 snaps me to attention. I thumb the crisp green bills, so happy to finally have money again.

"Since it was your first night, I put in a little extra," he says with a wink.

"You didn't have to," I answer.

"I wanted to."

Minutes float by before I realize that we're just sitting there, staring at each other in silence. Even though I know it's time for me to go, I can't seem to reach for the door handle, and Spencer makes no attempt to make me leave. At some point—it could be hours or even seconds later—he reaches up and touches my cheek lightly with his fingertips. I hear myself sigh as his hand grazes my earlobe, then slides behind my neck. As he leans in toward me, I feel my eyes close and my body go limp against him.

The second his lips touch mine, a cold, bracing shudder grips me. It's as if I'd just plunged into icy waters and the frigid cold is shocking me out of my dreamy haze. *What are you doing?* a voice screams inside my head. My eyes suddenly open with alarm. I turn my head to the left, feeling Spencer's soft lips slide across my mouth to my cheek.

"What's wrong?" Spencer whispers, nibbling at my ear.

I pull away. "I've got to go," I say, struggling to find the door handle in the dark. "This was a mistake."

"If it's about your boyfriend, like I told you—I promise I won't tell."

Taking the envelope, I slam the door behind me and walk off, without so much as even a good-bye to Spencer. My throat burns, as if I've just choked down battery acid and it's blistering my insides. Behind me, I hear the mechanical buzz of the power window being lowered.

"Call me tomorrow if you want to work," he calls to me from the car, "or if you have anything else in mind."

As soon as Spencer's Porsche zooms around the corner and out of sight, I knock on the window of the Escort. Kirsten unlocks the door to our new home on wheels and lets me in.

"Chloe said that was you in that sports car, but I didn't believe it," she says, pushing the seat forward so I can crawl into the back. "That guy really *is* loaded, isn't he?"

I lie across the back seat and curl up into a ball, clutching at my aching stomach. It hurts so bad, I'm starting to think something is seriously wrong. *Maybe the seat belt made my appendix burst when Spencer stopped fast. I'd better tell Kirsten to warm up the car. . . .*

"How far is the nearest hospital?" I groan.

Chloe clicks on the door light and stares down at me. "What's wrong, honey?"

"What does it feel like to have a ruptured spleen?" I ask weakly. "I think I have one of those . . . "

"Uh-oh," Chloe says.

Kirsten freaks out. "What? What's wrong?"

Sweat beads up on my forehead. "I think I'm dying."

"It's nothing," Chloe assures Kirsten. "Miranda comes down with a fatal illness whenever she's really shook up about something."

"I do not!"

"Don't make me rattle off the list of diseases you've thought you had," Chloe warns. "Scurvy, intestinal parasites, rabies, the bubonic plague . . . "

"All right," I shout, covering my ears. "Enough!"

Chloe hands me a bottle of water and crawls into the back seat with me. "So what happened that's got you in such a tizzy?"

I sit up to make room for her. "Spencer kissed me."

"Whoa!" Kirsten shouts. "Move over, guys, I'm coming back there . . . I don't want to miss any of this. . . . "

We all squish together in the back seat while I tell them about how Spencer flirted with me the whole time I was working the party and how the night ended in his Porsche. Saying the details out loud is so embarrassing. I must sound like the biggest bimbo in the world.

"I still don't know what you feel so guilty about," Kirsten says. "He's the one who tried to kiss *you*. He's the one who flirted with *you*."

"Of course you wouldn't understand," I snap. "Little Miss I-Can't-Stay-Faithful-to-Anyone-for-More-Than-Five-Minutes-at-a-Time."

Kirsten brushes her black hair out of her eyes and glares at me. "Hey, that was uncalled for, Chicky."

"Sorry," I say, holding my belly, "the pain has me on edge."

"Kirsten has a good point, though," Chloe says. "I mean, *he* pursued *you*. He was your boss, anyway—that's a little weird in itself."

"Both of you are missing the boat," I say. "I actually *liked* that Spencer flirted with me. I liked the fact that every time I looked at him, he was looking back. I liked the fact that he would go out of his way to notice me and fawn all over me. If I *didn't* like it, I would've done something about it."

"Well, what isn't there to like?" Kirsten argues, coming to my defense. "The guy's young, gorgeous, rich, has his own successful business—gee, he sounds a lot better than that jobless loser in Europe you've been stringing along," she teases.

"Not funny." I frown.

Chloe puts her arm around my shoulder. "Everybody likes attention, Miranda. Maybe you pushed things with Spencer a little far—but you stopped it before it got out of hand. I think that shows that you love Dustin very much."

"It was so hard to do, though." I cover my face with my hands. "I mean, his lips were . . . I should tell Dustin about this. I think I'd feel a lot better if he knew."

Kirsten imitates the sound of a missile dropping and exploding in midair.

Chloe shakes her head. "Not a good idea."

"Why not?" I ask.

"Nothing really happened, right? So why worry him just to make yourself feel better?"

I think about this for a minute or two. "But what if he asks me?"

"If he asks, tell him the truth," Kirsten says. "Otherwise, zip your lip."

I'm not sure this is the best advice, but at least it makes me feel better for now. I lean my head against Chloe's shoulder and sigh. "Listen to me, yaking on like this about my little problem after the horrible day you've had."

"I don't mind," Chloe answers, playing with my curls. "Actually, I'm tired of thinking about ballet—I'd rather talk about something else."

"Like where the three of us are going to sleep," Kirsten says. "So, which one of you is taking the trunk?"

The next two days bring funky, foggy weather, which seems to perfectly suit our funky, foggy moods. At first the three of us living together in the car seems like the ultimate in bonding experiences, but it quickly becomes a crash course in tolerance as the sleepless nights wear on. Soon, we start arguing over little things like which radio station we should listen to and whose turn it is to fetch fresh water at the grungy public water fountain in the nearby park. A few times it occurs to me that if I only worked a week or two with Spencer I would have enough money to find us a decent place to stay. But I just can't bring myself to go back, no matter how much money he'd pay me.

On top of everything, the standoff between Chloe and Madame has intensified. Kirsten and I are really tired of looking at the same old block of row houses, and want to park in a different part of the city, but Chloe refuses to let us move. She waits until a parking spot opens up directly in front of the house, then moves the car there. I think the goal is to make Madame feel horrible about kicking Chloe out and eventually wear her down with guilt until she practically begs Chloe to come back. So far, neither side seems even close to backing down.

Every day, just before Madame leaves for her morning class, Chloe gets out of the car and does some horribly embarrassing domestic routine right on the sidewalk to give Madame a sense of the hardship she's been enduring. Today, Chloe's taken her scheme to an all-time low, washing a bunch of underwear by hand and carefully placing the intimate items across the hood of the car to dry. From inside the car, I watch as the door to the house opens and Madame comes floating down the front stairs in a poufy skirt as black as her leotard. Madame, I've noticed, is just as stubborn as Chloe, refusing to notice she's there. Today, even with the underwear strewn all over the place, Madame walks by quickly, not even giving Chloe the satisfaction of a blink.

As soon as she's gone, Chloe scoops up the soggy underwear and slams it angrily on the ground. "I've had it!" she shouts, her teeth bared like a vicious dog. "I can't take this anymore!"

A few people have stopped to stare, but I manage to coax Chloe back into the car before we attract any more attention.

"Let's just get out of here," Chloe cries. "I'll go wherever you guys want to go—I don't care."

Kirsten wastes no time turning on the engine. "How about Texas?"

"Fine," she sniffles. "I don't care."

I reach over and turn off the engine. "You're not going anywhere, Chloe. You belong here."

"Obviously not—Madame won't even look at me."

"Have you thought of apologizing to her?" I suggest. "Maybe that's what she's waiting for."

Chloe freezes and gives me a horrified look. "Are you nuts? Whose side are you on, anyway?"

Kirsten looks equally appalled by my suggestion. "Yeah, what's wrong with you?"

"Nothing's wrong with me—I'm just offering a solution."

Chloe keeps on staring at me like I'm a psychopath. "What kind of solution is that? It's her fault, not mine! She should be the one to apologize—I'm sure as heck not going to do it!"

"Fine—live the rest of your life in a rusty old Escort, washing your underwear out of a bucket on the sidewalk." My voice is steady and calm, but inside I'm a complete wreck. "Madame's not the one who told you to buy those expensive clothes and spend all your time going to parties. She's not the one who kept you from paying your rent. You did that on your own."

"I can't believe I'm hearing this from my so-called best friend," she says, shaking her head uncomprehendingly. "I am *so* sorry I ever bought you that dress."

"I'm sorry, too," I tell her. "Had I known I was wearing a month's rent on my back, I never would've accepted it."

Kirsten wrinkles her nose in disdain. "That was harsh, Miranda."

"Stay out of it, Kirsten," I snap, feeling my blood pressure rise. Madame's words come back to me, and I decide I'd better just say what's on my mind. "Look, Chloe, I'm not going to tell you just what you *want* to hear—I'm telling you what you *need* to hear. You've got everything going for you, but for some reason you seem bent on ruining what you have. If you don't want to be a dancer—fine, I'm wasting my breath. But if you do, and I *know* you do, then stop messing around and get it together."

A dark shadow clouds Chloe's eyes. "You don't even have a clue about what to do with your life, Miranda—what makes you such an expert about what I should do with mine?"

"You're right," I answer, getting out of the car, "I don't know anything."

I slam the door shut and take a seat on the stoop outside the house. I sit in silent protest, certain that once Chloe sees how strongly I feel, she'll reconsider what I've said. But a few seconds later, the engine starts up, and Kirsten and Chloe take off down the street. I sit there for a long time, my heart swollen and sad, wondering if I'll ever see them again.

An hour later, I'm starting to think that Chloe and Kirsten might've taken off for Texas after all. But just when I start thinking about my last resort—calling Spencer—the blue Escort appears in front of the house again. The car barely comes to a stop before Chloe jumps out and comes running up the steps toward me. "One thing I've always disliked about you, Miranda, is that I can never stay mad at you for very long," she says, throwing her arms around me. "I'm so sorry."

"It seemed like a long time to *me*," I say, laughing, a tinge of nervousness still lingering in my voice. "I was pretty sure you guys *were* headed for Texas."

"We got halfway and realized we didn't have enough money for gas, so we turned around," Chloe teases.

We sit on the stoop without saying anything for a while, watching Kirsten try to squeeze the car into a really tight space. Eventually, she ends up bumping the car in front of her, then bumping the one behind, rocking back and forth until she's wedged in so tight, you couldn't pass a nickel between them.

"I hope you're not in a hurry to go anywhere," I joke, "because it looks like we're going to be here for a while."

"I really want to straighten things out," Chloe suddenly says, as though she's talking to herself. "But I'm not sure how to go about it."

I watch Kirsten get out of the car and slide across the hood to the other side. "Are you asking an aimless loser like me for advice?" I say, grinning.

Chloe punches me in the arm. "Come on—you know I was just being a jerk because I was mad. But I'm glad you told me to wise up. I needed to hear that."

"It's just so hard to watch someone waste their talent, especially when I'd give anything to have one of my own," I tell her.

"You *are* talented, though, Miranda," Chloe says. "I've always pictured you writing books or something like that. You seem perfect for it."

"Why, because I'm an antisocial bookworm?"

"No." Chloe laughs. "Because that's what you love. And you've always done so well in our English classes. You're a natural."

Kirsten drags herself up the stairs, with her hands jammed in the back pockets of her jeans. "Sorry we took off on you like that," she says.

I shrug. "I knew you'd come back. You're like a rash."

Kirsten smirks, seeming to take pleasure in the comparison.

"Okay, so how am I supposed to go about getting back on track?" Chloe asks. "Tell me what to do, Miranda."

"I don't know," I answer, "I think I've gotten too involved as it is—"

"Come on," Chloe begs. She squeezes my hand. "I don't know how to handle this mess. I really need your help."

I don't know how to handle it any better than she does, but a few little ideas pop into my head. The first goal was to get back into the house, which happens about a half hour later, when one of the older students comes back from her rehearsal. She's kind enough to let us in, and the three of us sneak back upstairs to Chloe's room.

Once there, I head straight for the closet, pulling out every item with a tag still on it—and there are quite a few. Kirsten helps me pack them up while Chloe gathers up all of her unopened makeup jars and packs them as well. Next, we go through her stuff again, this time weeding out the used stuff that she doesn't need. It's hard for Chloe. I can see her wincing every time I pull something of her closet, but she tries her best not to complain. She knows what has to be done.

The next step is even tougher for her, because

we go back to her favorite boutique to return all the new clothes she never wore and makeup she never used. While the sales staff adds up her returns, Chloe drools over the discount racks, her hands lovingly caressing the designer clothes. It makes me glad that we cut up Chloe's credit cards before we even got here. When the finally tally is reached, the three of us are stunned at how much the clothes add up to. The store credits Chloe's account, taking a big chunk out of her unruly bill.

After we finish in the boutique, we move on to one of the vintage clothing stores in Chloe's neighborhood to sell off some of her old clothes and shoes. A guy with a pierced tongue dumps the bags on the counter and starts sifting through the stuff while the three of us watch. Chloe picks up a blue sundress with little pink flowers on it. "I haven't worn this thing in years"—she smiles—"so I guess I won't even miss it."

The guy holds up a green cocktail dress. "Nice dress," he says, whistling.

"That's just like new," I tell him. "Give her a good price for it."

Chloe snatches the dress out of the guy's hands. "Miranda, what are you doing? I bought you that!"

"You could really use the money," I tell her. "More than I could use the dress."

"But you love it!"

I take it away from her and give it back to the

guy. "It's all right, Chloe. You can buy me another one when you're rich and famous."

Frowning, Kirsten reaches for the pile. "Hey, that's my scarf! I've been looking for that."

I slap her hand. "Not anymore," I answer, remembering how I dug through the trash to get it back. All it took was a few squirts of Chloe's perfume and the shrimp smell was covered up—at least for now.

"That wasn't so bad," Chloe says, stuffing a wad of cash in her purse. "In fact, it was kind of fun."

"If you think that was fun," I tell her, "you're going to *love* where we're going next."

This time, instead of barging in on Madame Krakinov, Chloe knocks. Clearly Madame isn't expecting us like she did last time, because she answers the door in a fuzzy blue bathrobe, with her long gray hair trailing down the middle of her back. I feel almost privileged that she lets us into her apartment, because I imagine this is a side of her that very few people ever get to see.

"It's not considered polite to drop in on guests unexpectedly without calling first," Madame says, putting a full teakettle on the stove. "Remember that."

Chloe's eyes begin smoldering, but thankfully she has enough restraint to keep her mouth shut. I'm silently glad we left Kirsten upstairs for this visit—I'm not sure she'd be able to do the same.

"Sit down," Madame orders. Chloe and I obediently take a seat at the kitchen table.

Humility is not something Chloe practices often, and I can see that she's having trouble, so I give her a jump start. "Chloe came here to tell you something, Madame," I say.

Madame draws her bathrobe around her and sits down. "Go ahead. I'm listening."

Chloe sighs three or four times and shifts in her seat. I tap her gently on the wrist to try to get her going, but she doesn't say anything. When I can't take the suspense any longer, I talk for her. "Chloe's been doing a lot of thinking about the audition," I began. "And she—"

Madame stops me short with the wave of her hand. "Now I *know* Chloe's got a voice of her own—a rather loud one, too. Perhaps she should use it instead of borrowing yours."

I fall silent while Chloe's face contorts as she tries to formulate what she needs to say. Still, nothing comes out. Madame leaves for a moment to attend to the tea, and also, I suspect, to give Chloe a chance to pull her thoughts together.

"I hope you've cleaned your room out thoroughly," Madame says, placing teacups in front of us, "because I expect the new ballerina to move in sometime next week."

Chloe's eyes widen. "Who's that?" she says suddenly.

Madame pours the tea. "Some young, pretty girl from Chicago. She's been an apprentice with the Chicago Ballet since she was sixteen. It was quite the stroke of fortune that we managed to get her. Up until now, the school no longer had any room for an additional student, but your quitting made the space available. I guess things do work out after all."

It's easy for me to see what Madame is doing here in trying to get Chloe's competitive drive revved up so they can start talking again, but Madame's tactics are completely lost on Chloe. Her face turns as red as a tomato. She's seething.

"Tell her to turn around and go back home because I'm not leaving," Chloe says. "I have no intention of quitting whatsoever."

"Oh? I hope you're not about to also tell me that you expect another audition," Madame says.

Chloe looks down at the wooden tabletop. "I know there won't be another one. I'll have to wait for the next round."

"Well, this is quite interesting," Madame says, taking a sip of her tea. "I'm not quite sure that I can tell that poor girl she's not welcome here. She's a very disciplined, hardworking dancer, and I don't see the advantage of picking you over her."

Chloe's mouth begins to twitch, and her eyes swell with tears. I can see she's nearing the breaking point. "Please, Madame, please let me stay. I'm sorry I was so irresponsible. I'll be more serious, more disciplined this time, I promise."

Madame swallows hard. "I wish I could take you at your word, Chloe, but I'm afraid it isn't enough."

"I thought you might say that," Chloe answers,

pulling a white envelope out of her purse. She hands it over to Madame. "Here's enough money to cover last month's rent."

Madame counts the bills, her gaze shifting from me to Chloe and back again. "You didn't give her this money, did you, Miranda?"

"No," I tell her. "Chloe sold her clothes."

Madame falls silent. My first thought is that she's trying to keep Chloe in suspense while she decides whether or not to take her back, but as the seconds tick by it occurs to me that Madame is deeply moved by Chloe's sudden turn. Finally, she stretches her arms wide and, without saying anything, welcomes Chloe back home.

Feeling like an intruder, I quietly get up and head for the door. Before I make it into the hallway, though, Madame stops me.

"A package arrived the other day for you, Miranda," she says, offering me a grateful smile. "It's in Chloe's mailbox."

"Thank you, Madame," I answer, quickly closing the door behind me.

Sensing that I'll need a little privacy, I take the package out to the car before I even open it. My fingers are so cold and clammy, I can hardly open the small brown padded envelope covered with postmarks from the United Kingdom. On the label, my name is printed in neat, angular letters that seem almost drawn rather than written. As I run my fingers over the label, it occurs to me that I've never really seen Dustin's handwriting before.

My heart thunders against my ribs as I reach into the envelope to retrieve the only item inside it: an audiocassette with no label. I hesitate for a moment, partly afraid of what the tape might contain, but also enjoying the anticipation. When I can hardly stand it any longer, I pop it into the car's cassette player.

"Hey Miranda, it's me, Dustin," the tape begins. His voice runs over me like cool water, both instantly familiar and refreshingly new at the same time. *"I arrived in London a few days ago and so far it's been great, but I miss you so much, you wouldn't believe it."*

"I miss you, too, Dustin . . . you have no idea."

"On the flight over I had a lot of time to think about what you said in the airport and it made a lot of sense, even though it was hard to hear. For all I know, you could've just been saying those things to get me off your back (he laughs) *but if not, I really respect your decision to take time to develop yourself as an individual first before becoming entangled in a serious relationship. For the record, though, let me say that I'll be the first one standing in line when you're ready."*

I sigh and smile to myself, twirling the silver rope ring Dustin gave me just before he left.

"So here I am in this incredible city and suddenly I realize that I've got a big problem. Everywhere I go, everything I look at, I find myself talking to you, like, in my head. No, I haven't lost my mind, if that's what you're thinking. It's just that there's so much I want to share with you that . . . um . . . " Dustin's voice trails off for a second. He clears his throat. *"Anyway, so I came up with this idea. I thought that instead of talking to you in my head, I'd put it down on tape, so it's kind of like you're taking a tour with me. I guess it's the only way you can sort of be both places at once. So sit back, close your eyes, and I'll take you to London . . . "*

I ease back into the seat of the car, closing my eyes like he tells me to. Twirling my silver rope ring around my finger, Dustin's beautiful face suddenly materializes in my mind, his eyes drawing me into their liquid depths.

"The first place I'm taking you to is my favorite part of London, just outside the Houses of Parliament along the river Thames. It's nighttime, and the air is pretty warm. You stand under one of the big globe lamps, looking across the black river at Big Ben, which is glowing with light. I want to take you on one of the party boats that cruise up and down the river, but you want to stay here and wait for the chime . . . "

A moment later, the Westminster chime gongs in the background. I bite my lip and laugh, tears springing to the corners of my eyes. The tape clicks, and Dustin's voice comes on again, this time near the fountains of Trafalgar Square. Then, onto the British Museum, Piccadilly Circus, the Tower of London. He takes me to a Sunday in Hyde Park, where people stand on soapboxes to rant about anything from politics to literature. We see the changing of the guard at Buckingham Palace and share a ham sandwich at a pub in Maida Vale. Dustin even takes me shopping with him in Camden Town for a pair of Doc Martens. For a while, I really feel myself slipping away as though I'm truly there beside him. The empty space in the middle of my chest that has been aching for him feels restored. I feel like a whole person again.

"It looks like I'm finally running out of tape," Dustin says. *"I'll be heading off to Paris in a few*

days and plan on putting together another one of these tapes for you. I hope that wherever you are and whatever you're doing, you're happy and getting exactly what you need out of life. I also want you to know that I love you, Miranda, and I can't wait to see you again. Hang on to that ticket I gave you. You never know when you might need it. . . ."

And then the tape cuts out.

"I love you, too, Dustin. . . ." Opening my eyes again, I smile. The longing in my heart eases as I realize Dustin and I have moved beyond the limitations of geography.

Letting him go on without me wasn't a mistake at all because I can see now that Mike was right: As long as Dustin and I love each other, we'll find a way to be together. I'm starting to think that maybe it's even one of the best choices I've ever made because it was a decision I came to on my own, without the help or influence of anyone else. And whether I decide to go to Yale, or to keep on traveling with Kirsten, or to go meet Dustin in Europe—or whatever I choose—that'll be fine, too, because I'll come to that decision on my own, when I'm ready.

What's even better is that I'm starting to realize that I don't necessarily have to have all the answers right now. Maybe life doles out the answers in little digestible pieces, feeding them to you as you need them. You just have to be ready for them when they come.

When I look at myself, I see someone very different from the person I was back home. It's not that my hair or eyes look any different (how much could they really change in a few months?), but there's something, well, new about me. When I think back to that scared girl on her way to New York who had no idea what awaited her on the road, I feel related to her, but different—like her older, wiser sister. If I could talk to her today, I'd tell her not to be afraid, that tons of amazing experiences were awaiting her, even though things wouldn't always be easy or nice. I'd tell her that there is no situation life can throw at you—a broken heart, having no money, living out of a car—that you can't handle. I ought to know.

I'm a survivor.

A few days later, Kirsten and I decide to leave. We were both toying with the idea of settling down in San Francisco for a while, and maybe getting an apartment together or something, but it just seemed impossible with the amount of money we're trying to get by on, and living in the car for a few more weeks until we made enough money for rent just wasn't an option. So we're heading for the Southwest, where we can skirt the rim of the Grand Canyon and see the Painted Desert. I can't wait. It's always been a dream of mine to go there, and I plan on making Dustin a tape so he can enjoy the trip along with me.

The other added benefit of skipping town is that we'll be giving Chloe some room so she can focus on dance with minimal distractions. She doesn't quite look at it that way, pouting as Kirsten and I get into the car. She thinks we're abandoning her.

"It's for the best, really," I say, giving her a huge

hug. "You'll be so busy, you're not even going to notice we're gone."

"Yeah, right," she says mournfully. "You'd better call me."

"I promise."

"And you, too, Kirsten," Chloe says. "I want to hear from you."

Kirsten gives her an unsentimental nod from behind dark sunglasses. A patented Kirsten good-bye. "No problem, Clo-babe. I'll see you around."

Chloe looks down at her feet, kicking stones under the car. "Do you think you'll be heading back to Connecticut anytime soon?"

"Eventually," I tell her. "I'm sure we'll definitely make it home for Thanksgiving if not before."

A relieved smile breaks over her delicate face. "So maybe I'll see you then. That is, if you're not touring Europe with Dustin or living in New York, writing the great American novel."

"Who knows," I answer, staring out at the vast blue horizon. "Just about anything could happen."